"For some reason, the fact that I am a single father has suddenly made me prime husband material."

Tip was confused. "But you just said you wanted to find a mother for Meredith! I would think that a bunch of available women to choose from would be just what you're looking for."

Until now, Rob thought that all he wanted was a nice woman who would be a good mother to Meredith. But the woman who would be Meredith's mother would also be his *wife*.

Suddenly, something inside him caught fire. Tip was everything he wanted, and everything he couldn't have. But right at this moment, only the wanting mattered. He took her in his arms. Then his mouth came down to join with hers.

"Not bad, Winfield," Tip said breathlessly when the kiss ended. "You ought to be able to conquer any eligible mother in town with that."

Dear Reader,

What makes a man a SUPER FABULOUS FATHER? In bestselling author Lindsay Longford's *Undercover Daddy*, detective Walker Ford promises to protect a little boy with his life. Even though that means an undercover marriage to the child's mother—the woman he'd always loved but could never have...until now.

Book 2 of Silhouette's cross-line continuity miniseries, DADDY KNOWS LAST, continues with *Baby in a Basket* by award-winning author Helen R. Myers. A confirmed bachelor finds a baby on his doorstep—with a note claiming the baby is his!

In Carolyn Zane's *Marriage in a Bottle*, a woman is granted seven wishes by a very mysterious, very sexy stranger. And her greatest wish is to make him her husband....

How is a woman to win over a bachelor cowboy and his three protective little cowpokes? With lots of love—in *Cowboy at the Wedding* by Karen Rose Smith, book one of her new miniseries, THE BEST MEN.

Why does Laurel suddenly want to say "I do" to the insufferable—irresistible—man who broke her heart long ago? It's all in *The Honeymoon Quest* by Dana Lindsey.

All Tip wants is to be with single dad Rob Winfield and his baby daughter, but will her past catch up with her? Don't miss *Mommy for the Moment* by Lisa Kaye Laurel.

From classic love stories to romantic comedies to emotional heart tuggers, Silhouette Romance brings you six irresistible novels this month—and every month—by six talented authors. I hope you treasure each and every one.

Regards,

Melissa Senate
Senior Editor

Please address questions and book requests to:
Silhouette Reader Service
U.S.: 3010 Walden Ave., P.O. Box 1325, Buffalo, NY 14269
Canadian: P.O. Box 609, Fort Erie, Ont. L2A 5X3

MOMMY FOR THE MOMENT

Lisa Kaye Laurel

Silhouette
ROMANCE™
Published by Silhouette Books
America's Publisher of Contemporary Romance

For Kelly and Steve,
two miracles who changed my life forever

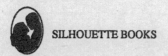 SILHOUETTE BOOKS

ISBN 0-373-19173-1

MOMMY FOR THE MOMENT

Copyright © 1996 by Lisa Rizoli

This edition published by arrangement with Harlequin Books S.A.

® and TM are trademarks of Harlequin Books S.A., used under license.
Trademarks indicated with ® are registered in the United States Patent
and Trademark Office, the Canadian Trade Marks Office and in other
countries.

Printed in U.S.A.

Books by Lisa Kaye Laurel

Silhouette Romance

The Groom Maker #1107
Mommy for the Moment #1173

LISA KAYE LAUREL

has worked in a number of fields, but says that nothing she's done compares to the challenges—and rewards—of being a full-time mom. Her extra energy is channeled into creating stories. She counts writing high on her list of blessings, which is topped by the love and support of her husband, her son, her daughter, her mother and her father.

The Logic of Motherhood

"Motherhood is not logical."
—Tip Padderson, mathematician and temporary mom.

If you want to play mommy, *then* hold baby close.

If baby cries anyway, *then* let her daddy hold her.

If her daddy holds her, *then* baby will coo.

If baby coos, *then* her daddy will smile.

If her daddy smiles at you, *then* you won't be able to resist him.

If you can't resist him, *then* you'll fall in love.

If you fall in love, *then* will you play his wife?

Chapter One

Things like this never happened, Tip thought with wonder. At least, not to her—Theresa Irene Padderson. But there it was, just up ahead on the deserted country road, with a lone shaft of late-afternoon sunlight stabbing through a rift in the angry clouds to point it out, like a rainbow leading to a pot of gold.

It was a phone. A phone booth, actually, the kind college students used to stuff themselves into and superheroes used to change in. Tip didn't know there were still any of them around, but after slogging to it from her broken-down car through a mile of Massachusetts mud in a downpour, she didn't care if she had to crank it. As long as it worked.

It didn't.

That was more like it, Tip thought as she slammed the silent receiver back into its cradle. Things like *this* happened to her all the time.

She didn't need to look a second time at the dilapidated farm stand next to the phone booth to know that it had been deserted for years, so she began to retrace her muddy footsteps. At least the rain had stopped, she consoled herself as she sloshed back toward the bright blue dot down the road. The adorable little sports car had seemed like such a good idea when she'd plunked down the last of her cash on it a week ago. True, even to her it was obvious that it had been around the block more than a few times, but the mechanic who had checked it out had assured her that the engine would run like a charm for years. If only the studly dimwit had paid as much attention to looking under the hood as he had to looking her up and down, Tip fumed as she yanked open the door.

Great. The convertible roof, apparently deciding to do its job as reliably as the engine, had allowed a puddle to form directly in the center of the driver's seat.

Tip kicked the door shut again and closed her eyes, wondering what to do next. What good was it to be running, when your car wasn't?

The sound of an engine filled the damp air. Tip opened her eyes to find a car had pulled up alongside her. At last, help. The driver, handsome in a distinguished way, was a man in his sixties with salt-and-pepper hair and a mustache to match. He smiled pleasantly at Tip as she approached.

"Looks like you could use one of these," he said, holding up a car phone.

She smiled back at him. "Thanks," she said, then hesitated. Other than that this part of Massachusetts was still a couple of hours away from her sister's house in Hartford, she didn't have a clue where she was, much less where to call to get someone to come and fix her car.

The man with the phone, sensing her dilemma, filled in the awkward pause. "There are two places in Madison you can try. One is a big towing place affiliated with one of those national automobile clubs."

Tip sighed. Belonging to an automobile club was a luxury her budget simply didn't allow. "What's the other one?" she asked.

"A repair garage owned and operated by a local man. Nice fellow." The man's eyes crinkled at the corners when he smiled at her. Although this phenomenon was commonly called crow's feet, Tip couldn't help thinking that the lines radiating from the corners of this man's crystal blue eyes looked more like sunbursts.

"Sold," she said, smiling back, and the man began dialing. He seemed nice enough, a grandfatherly type, and his recommendation of the local guy was all she had to go on. Not that it mattered much anyway, Tip told herself. In her experience, the guys who worked in those places were all the same anyway.

He handed her the phone, which rang about ten times before a gruff voice answered, "Yeah?"

"Is this, um . . ."

"Madison Motors," the man in the car whispered, smiling his encouragement.

"Madison Motors?" Tip finished.

"Who's this?"

The voice on the phone was abrupt. But since he didn't say no, Tip had to assume this was the place. "I'm a potential customer. My car is broken down."

"Damn. Where?"

His curtness was really beginning to annoy Tip. After all, the man was a business owner. He was supposed to be providing a service. And he was reputed to be *nice*. "Down the road from an old farm stand. Gray's farm stand," she added with prompting from the man in the car.

"How did you get this number?"

What was this man's problem? Tip wondered. She was about to tell him where to go, when she caught the eye of the driver of the car. She didn't want to repay his kindness with a display of rudeness. He had no clue as to how provoking the "nice fellow" was being on the phone.

"A *gentleman* passing by, who kindly allowed me to use his phone, recommended your garage," Tip said, and if she had placed emphasis on the word gentleman, it wasn't by accident.

"Who the—"

"Thank you for your help," Tip cut in. She was not about to grovel to get this guy to come help her. She would rather push her car to Hartford. "Goodbye."

She handed the phone back to the man in the car and smiled at him. "Thank you," she said.

"You're all set?" he asked, sounding relieved. Apparently her side of the conversation had led him to believe that the man from Madison Motors was coming to help her, which was exactly what she wanted him to believe. For some inexplicable reason, Tip hadn't wanted to hurt his feelings. He had been genuinely nice, even if a lousy judge of that trait in his fellow human beings.

"I'm all set," she repeated. And she would be. Eventually. As soon as another helpful person with a car phone came by so she could call that other place.

After all, it had only taken two hours for this first car to appear.

"Would you like me to wait with you?" He looked at her with fatherly concern.

"No," she assured him. "But thank you anyway."

He gave her a long appraising look, and absurdly, she almost confessed, like a child who wears the evidence of a cookie-jar raid in the crumbs ringing her mouth.

"Good luck, then," he said, and with another smile and a wave of his hand, he was gone.

Within minutes, the rain started again. In her hurry to get into her car, Tip forgot about the puddle and landed in the driver's seat with a splash. Groaning, she rested her forehead against the steering wheel. Plop. A drop of water from the leaking roof landed on her back. Plop. It was going to be a long afternoon. Plop. Evening? Plop. Night? Plop, plop.

Rob Winfield punctuated a long string of curses with the slamming of his tow truck door. He stared moodily out of the windshield while the engine warmed up. The truck hadn't been used in a while, and dammit, he wished he weren't using it now. It was Sunday, for cripes' sake. And so far, nothing had gone right. He had tickets for a baseball game, and at the last minute he had been unable to go. Not only had he been looking forward to getting away for a long time, but the reason he couldn't get away today was going to complicate the hell out of the foreseeable future of his already overly complicated life. At the very least, as a consolation prize, he should be left in peace at home so he could watch the game on television and sulk.

Or catch a nap. He hadn't seen much of the inside of his eyelids for the past few months.

Drops of rain began to spatter the windshield. With another curse, he turned on the wipers. From the look of the sky, it was going to be coming down for a long time. That road out by the old farm stand would be sheer mud by now. Why the hell had some woman been driving on a back road that was only used by the few families who lived on it?

And why the hell was he going to rescue her?

After a glance at the seat next to him, Rob put the truck in gear and swung out onto the road. He knew why.

Because he wondered who in the wide, wet world had given her his home phone number.

And because *somebody* had to rescue her.

And, all right, because his rudeness to her on the phone had been uncalled for.

He passed the old farm stand, and groaned as her car came into view. It was one of those toy foreign jobs that he hated working on, the kind that looked like you had to wind up a rubber band under the hood to make it go.

So why didn't he just turn around and go home?

Because she hadn't been rude back to him, even though she'd had reason enough to be. He couldn't deny that she had sounded, well, nice. He figured he had no choice but to meet her.

Because, for the first time in his life, Rob Winfield was solid in the market for a nice woman.

As she lowered her head to the steering wheel, Tip's brain went into overdrive. Her perverse psyche, ever ready to seize on a moment of weakness, had decided that this was the perfect opportunity to do something she had been avoiding for the past few years, and that was to Contemplate Her Life. Where She Had Been, and, since it seemed like there would be ample time, Where She Was Going.

It wasn't that she didn't know where she *wanted* to go. More than anything, she wanted a family. But first she had to find a man who would be drawn to her because of who she was, and not because of the damnable reason most men were attracted to her. One who would *love* her. And if by some miracle there was such a man, and she was lucky enough to find him, she wanted to marry him and have his babies, and bring them up in a close, loving family like the kind she'd grown up in. A simple dream.

And one that Tip had learned to stop dreaming.

Because five years ago, when it had been within her grasp, the dream had slipped right through her fingers. Somewhere between the marrying and the babies, she had blown it. Big time.

Now, not only did she not know Where She Was Going, but she also found it very difficult to care.

Where She Was Now was depressing enough. She had just quit her job in Maine, talked her way out of the lease on her apartment, closed her bank account and taken off. She should be used to this. It was the fifth time she had done it in as many years. The other times, she had gotten a wonderful sensation of escape. This time, the sensation she got was more like doom.

It would be nice to have a place to stay for cheap— or preferably, for free—while she regrouped. She could stay a few days in Hartford with her sister, but longer than that was out of the question. Mary Kate's fast-growing family already filled their house. She would move on, to...somewhere.

She hadn't counted on buying a car that was more comfortable with the concept of stop than with go. If it couldn't be fixed in a hurry, and cheap, things were going to look even worse for Tip than they did now.

Suddenly the passenger door was flung open. Tip jerked her head up from the steering wheel to see a strange man drop into the low-slung seat beside her and slam the door shut. Even in her shock, she found herself considering her options. She couldn't drive away, since the car wouldn't start. There was no use screaming or blowing the horn, since the road was all but deserted. And she didn't have anything handy that she could pull out and brandish at him. Unfortunately.

Because the man was large. Very large. Too large to be fully contained on his side of her car, the smallness of which was only now becoming fully apparent to Tip. Now that this man was sitting there with his shoulder wedged against hers.

She turned and plastered her back against her door, facing him with a scowl and a tone of false bravado. "Who are—" she started to say, no, *demand,* but just then a drip from the leaky roof landed right smack on her nose.

While she scrunched herself even further against the door, he had the nerve to crack a half grin at her expense. For the second time that day Tip found herself looking into the crystal clear blue eyes of a perfect stranger. But the other one, the older man who had let her use his phone, had been a perfect gentleman. This one looked like a perfect scoundrel.

It wasn't just the seen-better-days denim jacket and jeans that clung to his muscular frame, or the dark hair dripping with rain. It wasn't just the mocking tilt of his lips—lips that had the nerve to make Tip think about deep, wet French kisses—or the beard stubble highlighting a jawline that would send Hollywood producers into spasms. It was her absolute certainty, before he even said a word, that the gruff voice she'd heard on the phone belonged to him.

"What's wrong with the car?" he asked with that very voice.

She was right. Tip looked out her window and saw a tow truck with Madison Motors painted in faded letters on the door. It looked like a relic and probably made a racket, and she cursed her meddling psyche for distracting her to the point that had allowed it to sneak up unnoticed. She could have used a few spare moments to steel herself to talk to this man, before he dropped into her car.

"You may not believe this," he said after a few moments of silence had passed, "but I can think of things I'd rather be doing right now. What's wrong with the car?"

Just because Tip didn't know a darn thing about cars was no reason to let herself behave like the stereotype of an ignorant damsel in distress that guys like him expected all women to be. She summoned up all the repair garage terminology she had ever heard in her years of car ownership.

"What's wrong with the car?" she asked sarcastically. "I was just sitting here wondering that myself, and I can't decide whether it's a leak in the fuel line, or a faulty distributor cap, or if the spark plugs need to be replaced, or if the catalytic converter—"

"Are you sure you're the same lady who called me?" he interrupted her. "You sounded so nice on the phone."

"And you didn't," she snapped.

"I came here, didn't I?" he shot back irritably. Rob took a deep breath and struggled to collect himself. He didn't want to act like this. But he had clearly been caught off-balance, as much by her wide gray eyes and adorably tousled red hair as by her sass. The silence between them was filled with the roar of the rain, coming down with doubled force now, against the car's ragtop. He had to raise his voice to be heard over it, but he kept his tone deliberate. "Look, I know breaking down is no fun, and you've probably been here a while. What I was trying to find out was whether you were out of gas or had a flat tire or something."

He was being conciliatory, but Tip's temper had gotten the better of her and spurred her on. "Believe it or not, I am fully capable of reading a gas gauge, and on a good day, I have even been known to recognize flat tires on sight," she said. "It's the engine. It stopped running, and it won't start again."

"Rubber band probably broke," he grumbled as he went back out into the downpour.

Wondering if he was crazy, Tip watched as he got into his truck and backed it up in front of her car. When he got out, she did too, thinking that the one right thing she had done that day was to have her rain jacket with her. She yanked the hood over her head.

He was fiddling around in the back of the truck, clearly getting ready to hook up her car.

"Are you going to *tow* it?" she asked, incredulous.

He shot her a quick glance. "No, I thought if I whistled it would follow me back to the garage."

Tip tapped her foot in the puddle she was standing in. "I mean, aren't you going to look under the hood or anything? Can't you fiddle with some wires or something?"

He pinned her down with his laser blue eyes. "Let's get something straight here. I will not take advice about how to do my job from someone whose professional mechanical experience is limited to turning a hair drier on and off."

Tip looked where he was looking, and saw the faded bumper sticker that had been left on by the car's previous owner. It proclaimed, Hairdressers Do It With Style.

She drew herself up straight and looked right up at him, smoldering, ignoring the rain that was pelting her on the face. "On behalf of the hairdressers of the world, I would love to tell you to take a flying leap. Except I am not one."

He gave her a long look, and she felt a flush start at the roots of her hair, which was red and wild and the bane of her appearance, even when it wasn't damp through and squashed under a hood.

"So what are you?"

"Excuse me?"

"Are you by any chance a mechanic?" he asked with exaggerated politeness.

"I am a mathematician," Tip said firmly. She had never felt the need to impress anyone with her job, but for some reason she added, "I teach college-level mathematics."

He stood there in the downpour and planted his hands on his hips. "Oh, really? Well, then, add this up, Professor. I am a mechanic, not a 24-hour towing service. I consider myself more than a good sport to come out in this weather after being interrupted at home on a Sunday. I did it because you sounded nice on the phone, and even though you don't in real life, while I was here I thought I'd help you out anyway. I draw the line at standing in the rain listening to you tell me how to do my job."

Tip was silent, feeling she had been justifiably chastised.

He went on. "I am willing to look at your car in my warm, dry garage. If you have a problem with that, I'll be on my way."

Tip swallowed, wondering if she could handle a towing bill on top of a repair bill. At the same time, the last thing she wanted was for him to be on his way and leave her there. Even if the second to last thing she wanted was to go anywhere with this man.

"No, that's fine with me," she said between gritted teeth.

He looked at her for a few more drippy seconds before starting to string her car up. Several times during the process, he opened the door of his truck and looked in, then shut it carefully. Tip watched him, wondering whether she would have to sit up there with him or if she would have to ride in her own car, which was now tilted up at a ridiculous angle. She wasn't sure which would be a more unpleasant experience.

When he was finished, he settled the matter for her by opening the passenger door of his truck and motioning her inside. She climbed up, bracing herself to find heaven knew what manner of disgusting things inside it, then felt her jaw drop as she stared at the middle of the wide front seat.

"There . . . there's a *baby* in here!" she sputtered as he closed the door in her astonished face.

Rob walked around the front of the tow truck. Some judge of character he was. She had sounded so nice on the phone. Kind of polite and prim, like she was a real lady.

In real life, she was as spitting-fierce as a tigress. She even looked like one, with that red-blond mane of wild hair. And to top it off, she was an intellectual snob who clearly looked down her freckled nose at him.

He had been fooled by the sound of her voice on the phone. She was the right age—about three or four years younger than his twenty-nine, he guessed—but that was the only point in her favor. Far from being the kind of woman he wanted to find, she was exactly the kind he had to steer clear of. If he hadn't known it when she stood there in the rain arguing with him, he sure as heck figured it out as he watched her climb up into the cab of his truck.

Because when Miss Smarty Britches had reached up for a hold, her army-reject rain jacket hiked up enough to reveal a world-class derriere.

Damn.

Tip felt some of the slack leave her jaw as the driver's door opened. By the time he had slid into the seat she had recovered enough to repeat, "There's a baby in here."

"Yeah," he said absently, as if babies were standard equipment in tow trucks.

"Is it yours?" Tip asked.

He threw her a look of pure annoyance. "She is a she, and yes, she is mine. Did you think I kidnapped her, Professor?"

Tip found herself looking straight into those clear blue eyes. They were riveting. It was several seconds before she could speak. "That's not what I meant," she said, and it was several more seconds before she succeeded in pulling her eyes away. Then she looked at the baby, who was bundled into a car seat between them, and couldn't stop looking at her.

Admittedly, Tip adored babies. Her brother had one, and her sister had two, and Tip saw them as often as she could manage. But this baby—oh, how quickly and completely this baby captured her. She looked so small and fragile and sweet, lying there peacefully in the tense atmosphere of the truck, with two fringes of dark lashes resting gently against the smooth skin of her plump cheeks. As Tip sat there looking at this baby, maternal feelings that had never seen the light of day exploded within her, pressing out against her chest, begging for release. Tip wanted to touch the baby, to hold her, but of course, she couldn't give in to that impulse.

"She is absolutely exquisite," she whispered instead, her voice husky with reverence. She moved her gaze from the girl to the father, who was watching her look at his baby. She noticed for the first time how tired he looked, even though his blue eyes were alight with pride.

"Isn't she?" he said. His voice had softened, and so had his expression.

"What's her name?"

"Meredith. And I'm Rob, Rob Winfield," he said, reaching across the infant's car seat to offer his hand.

"Tip Padderson." Tip tentatively put her hand in his. Immediately, she found herself wondering how his hand could be so warm after he had been working outside in an unseasonably cool summer rainstorm. The contact felt so unexpectedly good that she quickly drew her hand back and cleared her throat. "Now I know why you kept opening the door and looking in here."

"She's usually down for the count after she eats, but I had to make sure."

They looked at each other, and this time Tip found she couldn't look away. Rob gave her a lopsided grin, and she felt what remained of her irritation dissolve.

"What do you say we start over?" he said.

"All right."

He started the engine and the truck went off slowly down the muddy road.

"Well, well," Tip said. Not exactly sparkling conversation, but she wasn't sure what to say to the man now. A few minutes ago, she had been spoiling for a fight, but his half smile and quasi-apology had effectively quashed her combative mood. She tried to piece together her two conflicting images of him—the ill-tempered, fractious one and the nice, fatherly one.

Stealing a sideways glance at him as he drove, Tip found that a third image, at odds with the first two, had forced its way into the mix. He was a handsome man. It was obvious where baby Meredith had gotten her gorgeous eyelashes. But something more than his appearance had Tip squirming in her seat with uneasiness. He wasn't merely attractive in an objective way, like a model in a magazine. She was attracted *to* him. And as soon as she admitted it to herself, she started to fight it. The pull she felt toward him was as strong as it was unexpected, and every instinct she possessed told her to dig in her heels and resist.

"How old is she?" Tip asked, both curious and glad to use the baby as a diversion.

"Four months."

"Do you often bring her along when you work?"

"No."

"But you did this time."

"I told you why I answered your call."

He had thought she sounded nice, Tip recalled. "I feel bad about your dragging this poor baby out in the rain."

"It wasn't raining when I left," Rob pointed out. He wasn't sure he liked her insinuation. "If it had been, you might still be on the side of that road."

"Still," Tip persisted, "why didn't you just leave her at home with her mother?"

He was silent. The windshield wipers rubbed back and forth across the glass, four times, five, six. "Her mother doesn't live with me."

They must be divorced, Tip thought. She felt unaccountably relieved, which annoyed her to no end. "Do you have Meredith on the weekends, then?" she asked.

"Weekends, weekdays, all the time."

What? A woman not wanting at least some contact with this adorable child was beyond Tip's comprehension. Unless...

She lowered her voice. "Has her mother... passed away?"

Without answering, Rob turned into a driveway. A number of cars were parked along the edges, and a garage building with three huge doors, one open, lay straight ahead. Madison Motors, the sign on it said.

Car Repairs, Domestic and Foreign. He still didn't say anything.

Tip couldn't bear the silence. "Am I being nosy?"

Rob pulled the truck into the open door and looked at Tip over the baby. "Yes, you are," he said gruffly, unbuckling the car seat with the baby still in it and pulling it out the door.

"And no, she hasn't," he added before turning his back and walking away. The way he said it, he made it clear that as far as he was concerned, her being dead would be preferable.

With a shiver, Tip slid across the seat and followed him along the cement floor of the immense garage. It was surprisingly neat and clean, like the inside of his tow truck had been. They were the only ones there, and their footsteps echoed in the large space.

Rob entered a room in the back, which apparently served as an office and a lunchroom of sorts, and put the baby, still in her car seat and still asleep, down on the center of a long table that had six chairs around it. He took off his jacket and waited as Tip shrugged out of hers.

Even though he showed no expression, his gaze made her uncomfortable. She had the feeling those clear blue eyes could see right through her.

Before she had finished peeling off her jacket, Rob had confirmed what he had suspected earlier, when she climbed into his truck. Tip Padderson had a body that would jump-start a dead man's heart.

But maybe that wasn't as bad a sign as he'd thought. Because to balance off a body made for sin, she had a healthy, glowing face, a sweet smile and wide, innocent eyes. He wouldn't make the mistake of judging a book by its cover. She may well be a woman of substance. Of character. The kind he was looking for.

She handed him her wet jacket, and he hung it next to his on a row of hooks behind the door. Then he loosened Meredith's hood, and Tip felt a catch in her throat at the sight of the baby's fuzzy head.

"She has red hair," she whispered. It was dark red, much darker than her own, but still it seemed to strengthen the bond she felt with the infant girl. She looked at Rob's hair, which she knew would be black even when it wasn't wet. "Where did she get it?"

Rob gave her that look again. Obviously, he considered this a personal question. Tip sighed. "Curiosity is my second biggest fault. I sometimes think I should have been a research scientist or an investigative reporter."

"Why didn't you?"

"Because of my biggest fault," she said seriously. "I can never stick with anything."

And that, Rob thought, was that. Nice or not, attractive or not, he was not in the market for a woman who blithely admitted that she had no staying power. Meredith had been left by one woman, and he'd be damned if he'd get involved with anyone who might leave his daughter again.

At his silence, Tip felt a little foolish. Why ever had she blurted out that very personal information to a man she had just met, and who probably couldn't care less?

Feeling flustered without quite knowing why, she added impulsively, "I haven't always been like that. Only after I got my—" Abruptly, she caught herself. With grim satisfaction, she realized that even five years after her divorce, she couldn't be flustered enough to bring up *that* subject. "My master's degree," she finished. "I've changed the topic of my dissertation so many times, I may never finish my Ph.D."

Rob still didn't say anything, just pulled a chair out for her.

That was brilliant, Tip told herself as she sat down. Now he thinks you're a babbling idiot.

Rob finally spoke. "From my mother's side of the family," he said.

"What?"

"You asked where Meredith got her red hair," he reminded her. "And while we're being nosy, I'll give you a cup of coffee if you tell me who gave you my home phone number."

"Right now, I'd trade you my car for a cup of coffee."

"That car? Ha. Even Meredith wouldn't fall for that, and she's pretty darn close to being born yesterday." He opened the refrigerator. "So who was it?"

"A man who was driving by. I never got his name. An older man, kind of distinguished looking."

"What kind of car was it?"

"Kind?" Tip blinked. "I don't know. It was tan, though. Or maybe white, with mud on it. I don't remember."

"Good thing you didn't become a detective. Not much of an eye for detail, Professor." The tone of his voice had warmed.

"Not professor. Instructor," she corrected him. "And I've told you all I know. Surrender the coffee."

He looked at her with a hint of a twinkle in his blue eyes. "Is regular all right? I don't have any decaf."

She nodded, thinking that a shot of caffeine was the last thing she needed right now. Her thoughts were already whirling around her brain at the speed of light. Turning on the coffeemaker, he cut into one of them.

"You must be worried about your car. As soon as this is ready, I'll take a look at it."

With a worried frown, Tip said, "I feel bad about ruining your day off."

He dismissed her concern. "We're here now, so I might as well check it out. The game I was going to watch is probably in a rain delay, and Meredith doesn't get another bottle till seven-thirty. At any rate, she'll snooze for a good hour or so."

"Well, thanks."

He gestured toward the desk. "You can use the phone if you want."

Tip smiled wryly. "I was kind of hoping I wouldn't have to. Like maybe it would be some silly little thing that you could fix right away, and I could just be on my way."

"It may be," he said, although the look he gave her showed he clearly thought it more likely that the car would sprout wings and fly away. "You can still use the phone, so someone's not worrying about you."

"No one is," Tip said softly. No one ever worried about her. The oldest child in her family, she had always chosen to carry her troubles on her own shoulders. And anyway, her sister in Hartford didn't even know she was on the way there yet.

Rob registered that one as he handed her a cup of coffee and took a seat across the table with his own mug. He had half wanted her to pick up the phone to call her husband or boyfriend, half dreaded it. But her tone of voice, as much as the words themselves, put an end to his wondering.

She looked over at the schedule board behind his desk and commented, "Busy place you have here."

"Yeah, I've got quite a week coming up."

"Who takes care of the baby while you work?" Tip asked, in a tone that she hoped sounded idly conversational. She was dead curious about Meredith's mother, for the baby's sake of course, but she didn't want to pry unintentionally again.

Rob put down his mug and rubbed the back of his neck with his hand. "That's a good question," he said, a trace of weariness in his voice.

"That's a lousy answer."

"It's a lousy situation," he acknowledged. "We've gone through four babysitters in the last two months. The fourth just quit today."

"What do you do to them?" Tip asked deadpan.

Most people would have taken that the wrong way, but Rob gave her that little grin again. A man for whom her sense of humor wasn't too dry? Tip felt her heart flop,

"Nothing. I was as warm and wonderful with them as I was when I met you," he said. Then he turned serious. "The truth is, they all left for greener pastures. I can't really blame them, either. The pay is lousy and there's no future in the job."

"Did they babysit at your house?"

He nodded. "I guess I just can't imagine taking my baby to one of those centers in the morning, and just leaving her there till evening. We live in that house right next door, and I come home to be with her at lunchtime. I'd hate to give that up. Plus I'm right here if there's some kind of emergency."

He captured her eyes again, and Tip felt her heart thud. This was not like her. Time had hardened her against the charms of men, but she could almost feel herself softening under his gaze. "So what happens tomorrow, when you have to work? Are you going to bring her *here?*"

"Don't make it sound like seven kinds of torture. If I have to, I will, but only while she's napping. I'll lose a lot of work time, but that happens every time I have to find a new sitter."

Tip wondered why she should be worried that he wouldn't find somebody good enough to take care of Meredith. "How long will that take?"

He shrugged. "The agency said this fourth one was the last candidate they had."

"Oh." Tip bit her lower lip.

Then Rob smiled at her. It was the first time she had seen his full smile, and it was a killer, with even white teeth that flashed in sexy contrast with his five o'clock shadow.

"Don't worry. We'll manage." He bent down to kiss the sleeping baby unselfconsciously, then disappeared out the door of the office.

Tip sat where she was, under the pretext of finishing her coffee. In truth, she was trying to get a grip on her scattered feelings. There was no denying the fact that this man, in some strange way, was getting under her skin. It was maddening, this side of him, with the appealing smile, the rugged confidence, the sound of his soft kiss on his daughter's chubby cheek. Tip could be drawn much too easily to him. Even though she was going to be gone soon—real soon, she hoped—that realization was troubling.

As she made her way to the sink with her empty cup, Tip saw something that caught her full attention. There was a calendar from a parts supplier hanging next to Rob's desk. Not that that, in and of itself, was so remarkable; after all, every desk in America had a calendar on it or near it.

This calendar, though, featured a large photo of a naked woman sprawled across the hood of a car.

Tip felt herself grin at her own expense. Had she actually begun to experience an attraction to Rob Winfield? How ridiculous. Because now that she had seen his calendar, her initial reaction to him came back stronger than ever.

He was one of those. *That* kind of man.

And that, thought Tip, was that.

Chapter Two

Tip spun around when she heard the office door open. "There's something I'd like to know," she said, crossing her arms.

"Something else, you mean, Professor?" Rob asked offhandedly. He leaned over the table to check on the baby, who was still asleep.

She ignored the jibe. "What I want to know is, what do naked women have to do with automotive repair?" she said, gesturing to the calendar on the wall behind her.

He looked at her as if she had just asked him what naked women have to do with sex.

"Never mind," Tip said, bringing a hand up to massage her temple. "How is my car?"

"At this point, I can tell you that you are definitely not going to drive it out of here tonight," Rob said. "I'll fit it into my schedule for tomorrow, though."

Tip didn't say anything.

He cleared his throat. "Unless, of course, you'd rather get it worked on somewhere else. In that case, I'll put it out on the lot so they can come get it."

"No, it's not that," Tip said, feeling awkward. "I just wondered how much this was going to cost."

"I'll give you an estimate tomorrow. No obligation."

"Thanks," Tip replied, then paused. "Heck of a job you've got, always being the bearer of bad news."

"Some people do tend to want to shoot the messenger." He reached for a clipboard from a shelf behind him. "Is your name really Tip?" he asked, pen poised over the paper.

"Legally, it's Theresa Irene, but no one has called me that since I gave Arthur Hasher a bloody nose in third grade."

He grinned at her over the clipboard. "I'll bet you gave the nuns in grammar school conniptions, Theresa Irene Padderson."

"Not on purpose." Tip grinned back in spite of herself. Insight like his could get unsettling if he started in on anything closer to the present. "Actually, I was far less trouble than my sister, Mary Kathleen, and my brother, Sean Patrick."

He gave her a look that said he doubted it. "Address?"

That was a toughie. Tip thought for a minute.

"I'll give you a hint," Rob said. "It's somewhere in Maine. Unless you have someone else's license plate along with their bumper sticker."

"I just bought the car a week ago, and I keep forgetting to take the bumper sticker off."

"You could just cover it with a new one. You know, 'Mathematicians do it...'" He leaned toward her, lowering his voice. "Help me out here. I never did it with a mathematician. How *do* you do it?"

Tip felt her face turn as red as her hair.

Rob grinned at her. "Speaking purely academically, of course."

He was teasing her. Tip made a quick recovery. "Are you really the moral guardian of that sweet innocent baby?"

Unoffended—again—Rob laughed right out.

"Have you remembered your address yet, Professor?"

"I remember my address," Tip said hotly. "It's just that I don't live there anymore."

"Where?"

"Maine."

Rob stared at her. "Let me get this straight. You just bought the car a week ago, registered it in Maine, and now you don't live there anymore?"

"It's a long story."

"The best kind."

Tip took a deep breath. "I left today. I'm on my way to my sister's in Hartford. I'll give you her address."

Rob wrote it down. "If you were on your way from Maine to Hartford, why weren't you broken down on the highway instead of on a back road in this neck of the woods?"

"It happened here because I was lost, but it would have happened on a back road anyway. The mechanic who checked the car out for me advised that I not go over thirty miles per hour."

Rob dropped the clipboard on the desk with a clatter. "Didn't that strike you as rather odd?"

"Look, I'm not real good with cars, all right? Obviously, or I wouldn't be here at your mercy. Now is there anything else you need to know?"

He looked at her for a few moments before answering. "Actually, yes. I'm assuming when you left your address in Maine you also left a job up there. Are you employed?"

Tip looked at the ceiling, at the floor, but not at him.

Into the silence Rob said, "Am I being nosy?"

Tip told herself he had more reason to ask that than she'd had to ask him about Meredith's mother. He was running a business, and he had every right to know if she would be able to pay him. "Yes, you are," she said, smiling faintly. "And no, I'm not."

"Sorry," Rob said. She must be having some run of bad luck. He could identify with that.

"Don't be. The college where I was teaching offered me a contract renewal. I left by choice," Tip said. "If there's something major wrong with the car, I don't know if I'll be able to afford to have it fixed. But I promise you that when you give me the estimate, I won't give you the go-ahead unless I can pay for it."

"I'll take your word. Now how about that phone call?"

Tip reached for the phone on his desk and tapped out a string of numbers. Maybe, just maybe, her sister would be able to make the two-hour drive to pick her up. She didn't know who else to call. She didn't know anyone in Massachusetts. Maine was even farther away than Hartford, and since she had only been there for a year, she hadn't gotten much past the acquaintance stage with anyone there.

Not that that bothered her. After all, she had learned the hard way that letting yourself get close to people was a particularly painful way to get hurt.

The phone at her sister's house rang four times without an answer, so Tip hung up before the answering machine picked up. No sense leaving a message that would only get Mary Kate worried.

"My sister's not home."

Rob, who had been finishing the paperwork, looked up. "Not home? Why isn't she waiting by the phone worrying about you?"

"She doesn't exactly know I'm coming."

"You were just going to show up on her doorstep?"

"What's wrong with that? She'd expect me to, and I'd do the same for her. That's what families are for," Tip said. "Don't you have a family?"

"Other than Meredith, not really. My mother died three years ago, and my brothers are scattered across the country."

"That's too bad. It seems to me that the situation you're in is exactly the kind a family could help with. Families should be close, and not just in miles."

He stared at her. "Did you grow up in a sixties sitcom or something?"

"Not really," she answered seriously. "We had our share of rough times, and maybe that's why we look out for each other. My mother died when I was in college, which left me kind of responsible for the other two. Which wasn't all that new, since my father died so long ago I can't remember him. What about yours?"

She noticed the muscles in Rob's jaw tense up.

"What about him?" he said.

"You didn't mention him before. Is he still living?"

"Yes."

"Isn't he close enough to help you out with the baby?"

"No." He and his father were miles apart. Changing the subject, he gestured toward the phone and offered, "If you'd like to try someone else—"

"Rob! Rob!"

The shout that came from out in the garage turned to a grumble as footsteps approached.

"Now where the H-E-double-toothpicks—oh, there you are!" A man of about twenty, wearing a flannel shirt and a backward baseball cap, charged into the office.

Rob planted himself in the man's path, hands against his chest. "Keep it down, will you, Ned? Meredith is sleeping."

"Sorry," Ned said. "But Fred's got the red tractor stuck in the mud down by the side of the road, and—" Just then he spotted Tip and took two giant steps backward, hit the wall and stood there, staring. "Sheeoot, Rob! There's a *girl* in here!"

"Yes, there is," Tip said, amused. "But I assume you already know Meredith. I'm Tip." She held out her hand.

Ned took off his hat and twirled it in his hands. "Pleased to meet you," he mumbled, without meeting her eyes.

Tip pretended she didn't notice that he didn't shake her hand, but instead poured a cup of coffee and offered it to him.

"Thank you, ma'am." He put the hat back on, and took the cup from her with hands that were noticeably shaking.

"Please, call me Tip," she said, smiling pleasantly.

Ned turned to Rob. "What's she doing here?" he whispered, fully loud enough for her to hear.

"My car died on the side of the road," said Tip, who was unwilling to be made invisible. "And Rob is going to bring it back to life for me. Now please, tell us about Fred and the stuck tractor."

Ned looked at Rob in amazement.

"Curiosity is her second biggest fault," Rob explained, straight-faced. "And she's probably not gullible enough to believe that your brother was out plowing in a downpour, so you might as well just spill out the real story."

Ned glanced at Tip, looked down at the cup of coffee in his hand as if wondering how it got there, and then spoke to Rob. "It was like this. The game was in a rain delay, so me and Fred got to talking about the tractors."

"They have two," Rob threw in for Tip's benefit. "A red one and a green one."

"You oughta see what we do at Christmastime. We park 'em in the front yard and string these twinkly lights all over them and—" Ned stopped as he realized he was addressing Tip directly, and quickly looked back at Rob. "Anyway, Fred was bragging that the red one could go faster through the mud at the side of the road than the green one could go *on* the road, and that green tractor is a honey, so of course I wasn't going to let that one go by. So the next thing I knew—"

"You were racing the green tractor down the road and Fred was stuck in the mud with the red one," Rob said, as if it could have happened to anyone. "And now you want me to tow him out."

Tip was glad Ned was too shy to look at her then, because she figured the grin on her face might hurt his feelings.

As it was, his face reddened. "Well, I wouldn't be in a hurry about it, because it was kind of fun to rub it in while he was sitting out there and couldn't go anywhere. But then the dang rain stopped. They're probably rolling up the tarp to get that game started right now, Rob," he added, as a last-ditch appeal.

"Oh, all right," Rob said with resignation. "I'm going to have to get the fool out of there before tomorrow anyway so he can come in to work. The new babysitter quit, so we're all in for a busy day."

"Shee-oot, Rob. Not again."

"Again." Rob moved toward the door. Ned followed him, and so did Tip.

"Can I come along and watch?" she asked, not bothering to hide her curiosity. You just didn't run across situations like this every day in the academic world. The potential for entertainment was too good to pass up.

"No."

"Why not?"

Rob turned around. "Because I figure that you owe me one. You can stay here and watch Meredith for me so I don't have to drag her out again."

Tip stopped right in front of Rob and tilted her head back so she could get a good look at his face. She assumed he was teasing her again. Anyway, she hoped so. She loved babies, but she didn't have a heck of a lot of experience caring for them. "You're kidding," she said flatly.

"Nope."

"You'd trust me with your daughter? You don't even know me!"

"I'm learning more all the time."

Tip just stared at him. He was serious.

"And anyway," he added, with a nod toward Ned, "I'm leaving him here to keep an eye on you."

"What?!" Ned, who had been hanging back with his hands in his pockets, listening to this exchange, suddenly took Tip's place in front of Rob. "You're leaving me here with her? Alone?"

"Promise you'll keep your lecherous hands off him?" Rob asked Tip, with a suggestive waggle of his eyebrows.

Tip sighed. She could see that she wasn't going to win this one. "Unless he begs," she said resignedly.

Ned's mouth dropped open, Rob laughed out loud and Tip headed for the baby. Then she stopped and held her hands out from her sides, palms up. "What do I do?" she asked Rob.

"Nothing. I'll be back before she wakes up."

"What if you're not?"

"Just do what comes naturally."

Tip looked doubtful.

"Don't worry. You'll be fine. And Ned will be right here by your side. Right, Ned?"

Ned looked as miserable as a human being could look. "Shee-oot."

Rob was still chuckling as he got behind the wheel of the tow truck. He hadn't laughed this much in a long time; at least, not with other grown-ups. It felt good.

He found Fred, gave him hell, and, finally, they got the red tractor out of the mud. It took longer than he'd thought, longer than he'd wanted it to. Rob didn't have a watch on, but he knew Meredith would be awake by now. He wondered how Tip and Ned were doing with her. He wondered how she was doing with them. He cursed the fact that, as the child of a single parent, Meredith would sometimes have to wake up to find her father wasn't there. He swore to himself he'd keep those times to a minimum.

As he headed back home, Rob thought about how Meredith's arrival had consumed his life. He had been living in a haze for four months. And that was right—that was how it should be. Caring for an infant took more physical and emotional stamina than anything he had done before in his life. He was proud of the job he was doing. He was a good father. No matter if Tip did make that moral guardian crack.

But in a strange way, this afternoon had been fun. Humorous adult banter, he guessed it was called. He wasn't sure he'd ever had the urge to tease a woman the way he wanted to tease Tip. See how far he could go before she turned that pretty shade of red.

Tip had brought out another urge in him. He had been physically attracted to her since he had heard her voice on the phone, and what he'd seen since had only made the attraction grow exponentially. With her wide, innocent eyes and the baggy clothes she wore, she might be able to hide it from an amateur, but he was a connoisseur.

He knew instinctively that Tip Padderson had a knockout body. The kind of body that, if shown to even minimal advantage, would stop traffic in any of your larger, more sophisticated cities around the globe. In a place like Madison, men would be stepping on their tongues.

Rob shifted a little in the driver's seat. On the one hand, he was relieved to be attracted to a woman in that way. It had been a long time since he had allowed himself the luxury of lust. Since the day Sondra had told him she was pregnant.

On the other hand, if he had been able to keep his hands off an attractive woman, his life would sure be different now.

But Rob Winfield loved his daughter, and he knew he wouldn't trade his life for anyone's. Not even for his own, the way it was before fatherhood. Interested as he was, intriguing as she was, Tip Padderson was just drifting past his life. She had no place in it.

Rob turned in the driveway of the garage, and immediately he didn't like what he saw. Or rather, what he didn't see. Ned's pickup truck, which had been parked out front when Rob had left, was gone.

Telling himself there was a logical explanation, Rob slammed out of the cab and walked briskly into the garage. It was eerily quiet, much too quiet for two adults and an awake baby to be inside. But they had to be there.

He flung open the door to the office. It was empty. His heart pounding, he stood for a minute, wondering what to do. On a hunch, he dialed Ned's number.

Fred answered.

"Where's Ned?" Rob growled.

"Hey, Rob! How come you didn't tell me you had a babe over there?"

"Is Ned there?" Rob's patience was holding by a thread.

"Yeah. What's eating you?"

"Put him on." When Ned came on the line, Rob exploded. "What the hell are you doing there?"

"Watching the game," Ned said.

"You're supposed to be here!"

"Well, when the game came back on the radio, Tip said she guessed you wouldn't be much longer and I might as well go on home so I could watch it. She's kinda nice, you know."

"How long ago was that?"

"Oh, about an hour ago. Baby was awake, but she wasn't fussing or nothing."

An hour ago. Rob counted to ten and said evenly, "Any idea where they might be now?"

"They're not there in the office?"

"Would I be asking you if they were?"

"I don't know where they could have gone, but don't worry about Meredith, Rob. That Tip, she's kinda nice."

Rob hung up on him and stormed next door to his house to get the keys to his Jeep. It was a helluva lot faster than the truck, and he was in a helluva hurry.

Charging up the back steps and throwing open the screen door, he noticed that the inside door was ajar. He went in quietly and paused in the kitchen. There was a bottle warming up in a pan on the stove. From the other room he heard Meredith cooing, and Tip's voice saying, "And this little piggy cried, 'Wee-wee-wee...'"

Heart pounding, breath ragged, Rob stood in the living room doorway and tried to absorb the peace of the scene before him. Meredith was lying on her back on the floor, smiling and watching Tip, who was stretched out next to her, holding one of her tiny bare feet in her hand. As she finished the rhyme, Tip tickled Meredith all the way up her chubby front, and they both laughed. To Rob, at that moment, it was the most entrancing sight and most wonderful sound on earth.

When Tip rolled over onto her side to face him, she looked incredibly seductive. Rob barely had time to tell himself that she didn't mean to, when she smiled up at him.

"Daddy's home," she said to the baby.

Rob just stood in the doorway.

All of a sudden Tip jumped to her feet. "Omigosh, the bottle," she said, pushing past him into the kitchen. Just walking by him, she got a rush of awareness.

He was broad-shouldered and lean-hipped and tall. She only came up to his chin. And he looked even better than she had remembered. She retrieved Meredith's bottle from the pot and held it out to him.

He was still staring at her. She took a closer look at him, and awareness hit. "You didn't know where we were, did you?" she asked.

Rob shook his head and went over to pick up Meredith. He hugged her close, speaking softly to her, and his breathing gradually slowed.

After a moment, Tip said, "When you were gone so long, I thought I'd come over here and see if the door was unlocked. Meredith was getting a little restless, and I didn't want to put her down over there. I left a note on the desk. I'm sorry you were worried."

"It's all right. I just didn't think to look for a note," Rob said, lifting his lips from where they had been nuzzling his daughter's fuzzy hair. "Ned and Fred and I always leave messages for each other on the answering machine, and that was clear." He should have guessed that her curiosity would lead her over to the house, with him being gone so long. And obviously, she had taken good care of his baby.

Tip handed him the bottle again, and this time he took it. "Seven-thirty," she said. "Wasn't that the time you told me Meredith got her next bottle?"

"You remembered." Rob sat down on the sofa, cradling the baby in the crook of his arm.

Tip sat down across from them. "It wasn't too tough. The schedule was on the refrigerator door, and the bottle was inside."

"I do them all in the morning. I like to be prepared."

Tip rolled her eyes. No kidding. Meredith's changing table had been stocked with every imaginable baby item, for any imaginable need. "Were you always this organized?"

"Only since I had a baby," he said, relaxing into a smile for the first time since he had come in. Meredith was sucking away at her bottle, looking up at him intently. "Did you get a hold of your sister?"

"Not yet." She went into the kitchen to try again.

"No luck?" Rob called when he heard her hang up. He was surprised to find that he was hoping just that.

Tip appeared in the doorway. "No."

Meredith was drilling her bottle, making little smacking noises that seemed to get louder as the silence grew. Rob took the bottle away and lifted the baby to his shoulder, rubbing her back gently.

"I guess I'd better use your phone book," Tip said.

"Be my guest."

Now *that* wasn't such a bad idea, Rob mused as Tip disappeared into the kitchen. Meredith burped, and he settled her back down to work on her bottle again, waiting.

Ten minutes later, Tip came back into the living room and plopped onto a chair, resting her chin in her hands.

Rob set down the empty bottle and wiped some dribble from the corner of his baby's mouth. "No luck?" he said, for the second time.

"Story of my life." Tip managed a wry smile. "There was a big wedding around here this weekend, and the motel in Madison is full up. So are the ones in the neighboring towns listed in the phone book. Do you have any ideas? I'm in a bind here."

Rob took a deep breath. "So am I," he said evenly.

She looked at him questioningly.

"You're stuck here without a car and with no place to stay. I'm stuck without a babysitter, which will make it hard for me to fix your car or anyone else's." He paused. "How about we make a deal?"

Of course she was curious. "What kind of a deal?"

"I'll let you stay here in the spare bedroom if you'll mind Meredith for me tomorrow."

Tip stared at him.

"It'll solve both of our problems," he pointed out. He wasn't sure where the idea had come from, but now that it had, and he'd shared it, he hoped she'd say yes.

Tip didn't know what to say. Of course, she should say no. You just didn't sleep in a house with a strange man. But what other option did she have?

Rob mistook the reason for her hesitation. "How about I sweeten the pot? If you watch Meredith for me tomorrow, I'll forget about your towing bill. You'll only owe me for the repair. Which, by the way, may not be finished by tomorrow."

Tip dismissed this with a wave of her hand. "Of course it will. You're the best mechanic for miles around."

"Where did you hear that?"

"Ned."

"What else did he tell you about me?" Rob asked, thinking that it might not have been such a hot idea to leave Ned with her.

"Nothing that makes me hesitate to sleep with you," Tip admitted.

He raised one eyebrow, and abruptly, Tip's face colored.

"That didn't come out right," she said quickly. Trust her to let go with the mother of all Freudian slips in front of him. He would tease her to no end about that. "I meant, to sleep in the same house with you."

To her relief, he let it go without a comment.

"So what do you think?" he said. "The bed in the spare room is pretty comfortable."

Tip hesitated. It sounded wonderful. It wasn't that late, but she was exhausted. And it wasn't like she had anything to do tomorrow except wait for her car.

"Clean sheets are in the linen closet in the hall," he said, with a smile of silent encouragement.

While she hesitated still, her stomach growled. Across the room, Rob heard it and grinned.

"You should be finished making up the bed by the time the pizza I'm about to order arrives," he added, standing up and propping Meredith on his hip.

Tip bit her lip.

Rob stood in the doorway to the kitchen and picked up the phone. "Pepperoni sound good?"

Just then, Meredith peeked over her father's shoulder at Tip and broke into a wide, toothless grin.

That did it. Tip walked over and ruffled the baby's fuzzy red hair. "Tell your daddy to throw in some green peppers, and he's got himself a deal," she said. Then she went to find the linen closet.

Chapter Three

The smell of coffee brewing lured Tip out of bed an hour before the time she and Rob had agreed she would officially take over Meredith's care for the day.

"Good morning," she said cheerfully as she sailed into the kitchen. Meredith, sitting in her infant seat on the table, beamed at Tip and kicked her feet inside her stretchy pink pajamas. A radio tuned to the news was on in the background.

Rob sat at the table, cradling a mug in his hands. "Didn't expect to see you up this early. I guess Meredith didn't wake you up last night."

He looks tired, Tip thought as she met his eyes. Then she looked at more of him. He looked *great*. The back of her throat dried up.

Tip swallowed twice before she could talk. "Did she wake up? I didn't hear her," she said, aware that her voice was higher than normal.

And with good reason. Awakening in the morning to share a breakfast table with a man was so incredibly intimate. Especially with this man. Rob had more masculinity packed into his muscled build than any two other men she knew, yet he carried it so casually. Which made all the more impact on someone like Tip, who had never been impressed by macho posturing anyway.

Struggling to distance herself from his appeal, she went to pour herself some coffee, conscious of his blue eyes on her from behind. When she turned around, he stared at her chest.

Tip moved quickly to the refrigerator, on the pretext of looking for some milk for her coffee, which she preferred to drink black. When she turned back around, he was still looking at her chest. She felt a slow burn start there and spread up her neck, and quelled the urge to pour her coffee into his lap. She hated when men stared like that. And it happened a lot. Tip had been cursed with a lot to stare at.

"That's not in Maine," he said, meeting her eyes.

"What?"

"The college on your sweatshirt. It's in Indiana, not Maine."

So that's what he was looking at. Tip gave silent thanks that her coffee, though lightened unnecessarily, was still in her cup and not in his lap. And she was impressed at his knowledge. "I worked at this one before the one in Maine."

"What about the one on the tote bag I brought in from your car last night?"

"That one is in California," she said. "Three, no, four years ago I worked there."

"And the one on your sweatpants?"

"That was the first one. Right after I got my master's, five years ago."

"Were there any in between the tote bag and the sweatshirt?"

"Yes. In Ohio. That one's on my T-shirt."

Rob leaned back in his chair. "So you've worked at five different colleges in five years." She hadn't been kidding. She really didn't stay in one place very long.

"Nothing wrong with that math," she said, sipping her coffee. "Now on to more interesting subjects. Where is your newspaper?"

"I don't get a paper."

She couldn't believe it. "How do you get your news?"

"From that," he said, gesturing toward the radio.

Tip was a big fan of public radio, but right now she wanted to find out more about the tiny Massachusetts town where she had landed. "How do you get the local news?"

He gave a brief laugh. "What news there is in this little town comes in loud and clear over the grapevine."

"Not exactly a reliable source. Is there a local paper?"

"Yep. You can get one up at the variety."

"The what?"

"The variety store. It's about a half mile up the road, that way," he said, pointing over his shoulder. "If you leave now, you'll have time to walk there and back before you take over with Meredith."

"Actually, I think I'll take her there with me."

"Take her?"

Tip looked at him. "It didn't come up last night, but you do have a stroller, don't you?" After the pizza, he had spent an hour giving her carefully detailed information about Meredith's care and schedule, gone through a diaper change and bath with her and shown her where every baby supply in the house was kept. He had treated her like a new employee, and she was grateful for that, Tip reflected. It had made an evening that might otherwise have been more than a little awkward easier for them both.

"It's in a box on the porch."

Tip pulled back the curtains to take a look. "A sealed box," she said. "You mean you've never used it?"

"Guess not."

"Any particular reason for that? I mean, babies and strollers kind of go together."

"No reason, except I don't have much reason for going up to town." And he liked to stay away from the gossip chain.

"Well, as long as you have no objection, we'll use the stroller. I walk for exercise anyway. I'll love the company, and you, little lady, will love the fresh air and sunshine." She made a funny face at Meredith, and got the smile she wanted. Those smiles were addicting.

"She needs to be dressed," Rob said.

"Let me do it," Tip said, lifting the baby into her arms. "If you see me handling her before you leave, maybe you'll feel better about her being with me today."

"I'm fine with that," Rob assured her as he followed her down the hall. He wasn't sure why, but he trusted Tip instinctively. Just like, instinctively, he had wanted to wrap his arms around her and give her a good-morning kiss when she walked into the kitchen. Funny, he had never had that urge with Sondra.

"I love what you've done with her room," Tip said, putting Meredith into the crib while she gathered up fresh clothes and a diaper. It was sunny, and freshly painted a cheery yellow. The gray carpet looked new, too, and the furniture was white and built along classic lines that, except for the crib, would take Meredith from babyhood to girlhood.

"Thanks. I wasn't sure what I was doing when I picked everything out, but it seems to work well. Actually, I redid the whole house when I found out she was on the way."

That explained the updated kitchen and bathroom in what was clearly a 1940s-era ranch house. The place was small—just the three bedrooms, living room, kitchen and bathroom—but plenty big enough for the two of them, and with plenty of room to add on. Tip wondered again about Meredith's mother.

But not for long. She found out quickly that washing up, diapering and dressing an active and curious four-month-old was a job that required no less than full concentration. "I thought babies were supposed to just lie there," she said in frustration as Meredith wiggled and kicked.

Rob laughed. "I thought the same thing. I thought things would be pretty boring until she was old enough to walk and talk."

Meredith squealed and shook the rattle Tip had given her to hold as a distraction. Tip snapped the last snap on her little denim overalls with satisfaction.

"Did you see that?" Rob asked suddenly.

"What?"

"Meredith switched the rattle from one hand to the other!"

"Is that good?"

Rob picked his baby up and kissed her. "She's never done it before," he said. "Probably has something to do with that left and right side of the brain stuff. You ought to know, Professor."

"I told you, I'm an instructor, not a professor."

Maybe if you stayed somewhere long enough, you would be, Rob thought.

"Congratulations, Meredith." Tip playfully shook the hand with the rattle in it, and Meredith took advantage of the opportunity to grab a fistful of her hair with the other. "Ouch!"

Rob helped Tip extricate Meredith's little fingers from her hair. "You know, reaching and grabbing are important developmental steps too," he teased.

"I may not know much about child development, but I know a happy kid when I see one," Tip said, as Rob handed the baby over to her. Meredith settled in on her hip. It felt good. "You must be doing something right, Daddy."

He gave her that wide smile again, the one with those flashing white teeth. "Thanks," he said, and looked like he meant it.

By the time the two of them had set up the stroller, it was time for Rob to go to work. He gave Meredith a hug and buckled her in.

Tip ran her fingers through the wild waves in her hair. "Which way?" she asked.

"That way. Just stay right on this road, and it'll be on the first corner. Even you couldn't get lost," he said with a grin.

"Just don't go calling the cops if we're not back in precisely twenty-three minutes. It's a nice day, so we'll probably do a little exploring around town. I promise I'll have her back for her midmorning nap."

Rob watched her wheel the stroller up the street. Funny thing was, he wasn't a bit worried. And that was a first for him. He had never really liked leaving Meredith with a sitter. But Tip was different. Handling a baby was obviously not an everyday experience for her, but she asked questions if she didn't know something, and her instincts were good. Meredith would be fine, he thought, walking toward the garage.

He, on the other hand, was not fine at all. His attraction to Tip was growing by leaps and bounds. Even the bulky gray collegiate sweats she was wearing didn't lessen her appeal. She wasn't what most people would consider classically beautiful, but she had a pretty, wholesome face. He smiled. He liked her style, just running her hands through her tousled red hair and going out to meet the town of Madison. Sondra wouldn't even emerge from the bathroom without five pounds of makeup and ten of hairspray.

His smile turned to a frown, as it always did when he thought of Meredith's mother. Tip may be as different from Sondra as day and night in looks, brains and temperament, but they were exactly the same in one major way.

They were both leavers.

Tip Padderson was not at all the kind of woman he was looking for, even if he was attracted to her. Rob was glad she would be gone by the end of the day.

The variety store lived up to its name. Tip had never seen such a variety of goods crammed into such a small place. The shelves held everything from hedge clippers to dental floss. Along the back wall was a combination bakery and deli counter complete with a sign that boasted the best sandwiches in town. There was a serve-yourself coffee machine next to an old-fashioned wooden pickle barrel.

Tip was glad she had left the stroller outside when she saw how cramped it was inside. She shifted Meredith over to her hip when she reached down to take a newspaper from the pile on the floor. She plunked it on the counter. The morning rush, if there was one, was apparently over. The only customer besides her was playing the video game in the corner.

A middle-aged woman with a perm and a paunch strolled up behind the counter to take Tip's dollar. "Gonna play your number, hon?" she asked.

Tip realized she was talking about a lottery number. "Why not?" she said. She wasn't usually a gambler, but she figured her luck was due to change, so why not cash in?

While Tip fished for another dollar, the woman smiled at Meredith. "Cute kid," she said. "You must not be from around here. I'd have remembered this little doll."

Tip figured the woman didn't recognize Meredith without Rob. She decided not to get into explaining the situation. It could take hours. So she just smiled and thanked her and turned to go.

But instead of walking out the door, she went to the corner of the store. The man bending over the video game looked familiar.

"Ned?" she said, coming up behind him.

He jumped about a mile and spun around. "Shee-oot," he said, leaning back against the machine. "What'd you go and scare me like that for?"

Tip looked at the machine, which was emitting noises like electronic death. "What's happening?" she asked, her eyes wide.

"I am crashing and burning, that's what's happening," he said. "And I was having my best round ever, too. Thought I might break the record."

He must be pretty upset, to put so many words together in a row like that. He hadn't said as much in the whole hour he'd been with Tip the afternoon before. On the machine was a spot for the record score, which was held by Fred. She might have guessed.

"How come you're not at work?"

"Fred's in there now. He does the drop-offs. I stay late and do the pick-ups. That's so Rob can be with Meredith more. How come she's with you?"

Meredith was beaming at him. "I'm watching her for Rob today, so he can fix my car. Will you hold her?" Tip asked. "My arms are getting tired."

Ned held up his hands and backed away. "No way. I don't know how. If I dropped her, Rob would kill me or fire me or something."

Tip smiled. "Then would you take the paper for me?"

He took it and followed her to the door. Next to it there was a bulletin board filled with handwritten three-by-five cards, just the sort of thing Tip couldn't resist looking at. There were refrigerators for sale, meeting notices, appeals by enterprising kids who would mow lawns and shovel snow and walk dogs, and help-wanted requests, mostly for babysitters.

Apparently Rob wasn't the only one having a hard time finding one.

She was studying a list of offerings at the town recreation center when Ned cleared his throat nervously.

"I'd like to get another game in, before work."

"Sorry. I get absorbed sometimes." Tip went outside and buckled Meredith in the stroller. Ned handed her the paper, which fit nicely on the storage rack under the seat. "Thanks," she told him. "Maybe I'll see you later, at the garage."

He turned white, as if he hadn't thought about maybe seeing her yet again.

"Maybe," he said, then went back into the store with relief written all over him.

Out at the street, Tip made a point of looking both ways, but there was no question which direction she would head. To the right was a country road much like the one she had just walked up. To the left was an interesting-looking collection of buildings that must be the town of Madison.

"Let's see what there is to see," she said to Meredith, turning left. Next to the variety store was an old movie theater, a package store and the pizza shop where last night's dinner must have come from. Across the street, between the town common and an ancient cemetery, was the Madison Congregational Church with the regulation white clapboard sported by most of the old churches in the region. In the middle of the common stood a statue commemorating the soldiers of Madison. On the other side was the town hall, and beyond it, the library.

It was all a little run-down, but charming nonetheless, in the way Tip found all old New England towns. She took a right after the library. On the block behind the main street were a number of old homes, most of them large, with wide front porches and big old trees shading them. It looked like a nice place to live, if a little deserted at that time of morning. Few cars went by, and even fewer people.

Then Tip heard footsteps overtaking her from behind. She turned, and saw another familiar face. It was the man who had stopped to let her use his car phone yesterday. Wearing a T-shirt, shorts and running shoes, he looked like he had just finished his morning jog.

He smiled when he caught up with her. "I thought that was you! How's the car?"

"Rob Winfield is going to fix it for me. Thanks for recommending him."

The man's blue eyes flashed. "I'll bet you're glad you didn't have this little one with you when you broke down in the rain."

He bent down to look Meredith in the eye. "Hi, punkin," he said. "How old is she, Mom, about four months?"

"Yes, exactly." Tip was impressed. "But I'm not her mother."

He stood up again. "Must have been the red hair that fooled me."

"I'm just taking care of her while Rob fixes my car."

"She's from around here? Can't believe I've never seen her before. Is she the daughter of a friend of yours or something? It must be an inside job, for you to have gotten it in less than twenty-four hours."

"You could say that," Tip said, smiling. "I'm literally watching her for Rob so he can fix my car."

His smile slowly faded, to be replaced by a look of bewilderment. "For Rob? This is *Rob's* baby?"

"Yes," Tip said, surprised at his reaction. "I gather not many people around here have met Meredith, though I really can't imagine why."

The man's expression turned grim. "I can," he said softly. Then he seemed to recover and remembered his smile, which was just as pleasant as before, if a tad less genuine. "I've got to get to work now," he said, heading off in the opposite direction.

Tip watched him go. "Have you noticed the people in this town are a bit quirky?" she said to Meredith as they headed back toward Rob's house. The baby looked up at her and yawned.

Back home, Tip tucked Meredith into her crib for a nap. After a quick shower, she tried calling her sister again. This time, she got through.

"Tip! At last!" Mary Kate said. "I've been calling your apartment all morning. Where have you been?"

"Me? Where have *you* been? I kept calling yesterday and getting no answer."

"Tommy and I decided to take the kids to the beach for the weekend. It was a spur-of-the-moment thing. We stayed with that friend of his from college. You know, the one I tried to fix you up with."

"Mary Kate, which of Tommy's friends haven't you tried to fix me up with?"

"Funny. Now tell me why I keep getting a recording that says your phone has been disconnected."

"For a little sister, you sure can be bossy," Tip grumbled. "I moved, that's why."

"Moved! Again? Tip, no!"

"Gee, thanks for the support."

Mary Kate sighed. "Where are you this time?"

"Well, actually, I'm not anywhere."

"What?"

"I mean, I was on my way somewhere, but now I'm here."

"Where's here?"

"Madison, Massachusetts."

"Where's *that?*"

Tip massaged the back of her neck. "It's where my car decided to die yesterday on the way to your house," she said wearily, stretching the phone cord around the corner into the living room and plopping down onto the couch. "Don't bother looking it up on a map. I doubt there are any detailed enough to include it."

"Wait." Mary Kate was putting two and two together now. "Did you say you were on your way here?"

"I was wondering if I could stay with you guys for a few days."

"Well, of course, but...does this mean you quit your job in Maine, and you don't have another one?"

"Not yet," Tip admitted. "But it won't take me long to find one," she added quickly.

"It never does," Mary Kate said gloomily.

"Why do you sound like that? You should be happy that your sister is so marketable."

"I'd be happier if you were a little less portable. Tip, when are you ever going to settle down?"

"Maybe the next time," Tip said brightly.

Mary Kate wasn't fooled. "I'll believe it when I see it," she grumbled. "So when will you get here?"

"I'm not sure. My car is in the shop even as we speak. It could be ready now. But at any rate, I'll be staying here in Madison until the end of the day."

"Why?"

"I've got a babysitting job."

Mary Kate laughed.

"What's so funny?" Tip asked.

"You. You must be joking."

"Must I? The baby's taking a nap right now, or I'd get her to drool into the phone to convince you."

"But you don't know anything about babies."

"I do now."

There was a pause. "You're *serious?*"

"Why would I make up a story like that?" Tip asked.

"Why would a college instructor with an M.S. in mathematics take a babysitting job?" Mary Kate shot back.

Tip bristled. "Is this my sister I'm talking to, or one of the academic snobs I've been working around for the past five years?"

"A good point, but not an answer."

Tip felt an odd sort of pride in her little sister's feistiness, although at the moment she wished it were directed somewhere other than at her. "The baby's father is the one who rescued me from the side of the road yesterday. He's in a bind. His babysitter quit without notice. I figured if I helped him out, he'd fix my car quicker."

"Where are you?"

"At his house."

"Hmm. Where's the baby's mother?"

"She doesn't live here."

"Hmm. Where did you stay last night?"

"Here."

There was dead silence on the line. Tip could just imagine the connections being made in her sister's computerlike brain. Then Mary Kate nearly short-circuited. "Theresa Irene Padderson, are you telling me you spent the night in a house with a strange man?" she screamed.

Tip held the phone away from her ear. "He's not strange," she argued. "He—"

"Tip, where is your brain? He could be a rapist, or an ax murderer, or some kind of psycho!"

"He's not. Mary Kate, he's the father of a four-month-old baby girl!"

"Oh, like the fact that he can get a woman pregnant automatically qualifies him for sainthood or something."

Tip sighed. "Calm down, Mary Kate. I made it through the night, alive and untouched. You know I wouldn't have stayed here if he didn't seem trustworthy. And to tell you the truth, he's much too attractive to have to force himself on a woman."

Mary Kate's tone of voice underwent a complete transformation. "Oh, so *that's* it," she said, suddenly sounding annoyingly like she used to when she was a bratty younger sister. "You're attracted to him."

"There's a difference between attractive and attracted to. He is not my type *at all.*"

"Attractive. Available. Didn't try to take advantage of you last night. Sounds like everyone's type to me."

Tip felt her frustration level start to go off the dial. Her sister was clearly grabbing on to this idea, and Mary Kate had a hold like a bulldog.

"Don't be ridiculous, Mary Kate," she said. "For one thing, he's not the least bit interested in me." Men were never interested in her, except on the most basic, superficial level.

"Who's being ridiculous? How can you—"

Tip cut her off. "And for another thing, I'm not interested in him. Or any man."

That silenced Mary Kate. It was a few minutes before she said, softly, "Tip, when are you going to put your marriage behind you?"

Tip didn't say anything. She had been trying to put her marriage—and divorce—behind her for five years now. Funny thing was, the faster she tried to run from it, the tighter the past seemed to cling.

Despite Tip's silence, Mary Kate wasn't ready to abandon the subject. "It's so frustrating to know you've been unhappy, but not to understand why. Maybe if I knew the full story, I could help. I only met Michael the one time, at your wedding. Talk to me, Tip," she implored. "What happened?"

Tip sighed. "I've told you a hundred times. We weren't...compatible."

That was the truth, if not the whole truth. But Tip found it impossible to admit to anyone but herself that the marriage had gone up in smoke because of her. Especially to the little sister who had always looked up to her as a role model. Mary Kate, serenely happy as a wife and mother, didn't need the burden of knowing that Tip had been such a spectacular failure as a wife that she couldn't even hold her marriage together.

"So the two of you weren't compatible. Fine. Does that mean you can't go out and find someone else? Not every man in the world is like your ex-husband." Mary Kate paused. "Maybe this one isn't."

"Get real, Mary Kate," Tip said irritably, tiring of the argument. "I'm just passing through here, remember? And anyway, he's got one of those naked women calendars in his office, so he's not exactly Mr. Wonderful.''

Just then she heard a noise in the kitchen. Without a word, Rob came through and headed down the hall. Tip cringed. She hadn't even heard him come in. She wondered how much he had overheard.

"Look, Mary Kate. I've got to go," she said quickly. "I'll call back when I find out about my car, to let you know when to expect me."

After she hung up, Tip walked to Meredith's room. Rob was leaning over her crib, watching his baby wriggle and yawn and stretch and, finally, open her eyes and smile at him.

Tip stood in the doorway. "Hi. You're home for lunch, I take it."

He kept his eyes on Meredith. "Yes. And I take it you finally got through to your sister?"

"Yes, but don't worry. I reversed the charges, so it won't show up on your phone bill or anything."

"That's not why I asked."

"Well, she knows where I am now. They were away for the weekend, so I guess it's a good thing I didn't just show up there yesterday."

He didn't say anything more, so she filled in the silence. "How about lunch? I make a mean tuna sandwich."

He looked at her, his blue eyes clouded. "Cooking for me is not part of our deal."

"You call a tuna sandwich *cooking?*" Tip asked. "Anyway, it's your food I'm eating, remember? I'll call you when it's ready."

During lunch, neither one of them made further mention of her phone conversation. Rob told her that her car was next up and asked about Meredith. Tip told him about their walk and about seeing Ned at the variety store.

"You'll never believe who else I ran into," she said. "The man who stopped to help me yesterday. I guess this is what small-town life is all about."

Rob stopped chewing. He knew exactly who had helped her the day before. Not many people had his home number, which was unlisted, and even Tip's vague description of the man had been enough to confirm Rob's suspicions. "Did you talk to him?"

"Yes. He was out running. He stopped to ask how my car was and to shower compliments on your baby."

"Did he ask whose she was?"

Tip looked at him. "It was kind of a natural topic of conversation."

"Did you tell him?"

"Well, of course. It's no big secret, is it?"

Rob finished his drink and cleared his dishes. "What did he say?"

"Nothing, really. He had to get to work, so he went off in a hurry." Tip frowned. "Given how polite he was yesterday, I was a little surprised that he was so abrupt."

"I'm not," Rob muttered, and that was the end of it. After he fed Meredith her bottle, he left.

Tip gave a sigh, but not of relief. She held Meredith up to the window to watch Rob walk across the grass to the garage. "You may not believe this, but people think *I'm* complex," she said to the baby.

Meredith made a furrowed-brow face that Tip fondly imagined to be a gesture of feminine understanding. Then she promptly deposited her lunch all down the front of Tip's shirt.

Chapter Four

Later that afternoon, Tip strapped Meredith into her stroller and went over to the garage.

The first person she saw was Ned, bent over the hood of a car the way he had been bending over the video game that morning. Feeling devilish, she went up behind him and said, "How did you make it through the day without me?"

To her surprise, he turned around, looked her up and down brazenly, then leaned casually against the fender of the car. "The question is, how did you make it through the night without me, doll?"

Tip's mouth dropped open. Before she could say anything, the real Ned came over from the next bay, his face a dull red. "You leave her alone, Fred," he warned.

Fred ignored him. "You must be Rob's new girl," he said to Tip, with a wolfish smile.

She gritted her teeth. "I'm Meredith's babysitter for the day. And you must be the boy who plays games with tractors in the mud."

"Ooh, a feisty redhead. Just the way I like 'em. I'll take you on any day, doll."

"He calls me doll one more time and you'll see him get his wish," Tip muttered to Meredith as she pushed the stroller away. She had made more than one man sorry about coming on to her like that. But some battles were just not worth fighting, especially since she would be driving away from this place in hours.

On the other side of the garage, Rob was working underneath a car. "Special delivery!" Tip said, as she set the brakes on Meredith's stroller.

Rob wiped his hands on a rag and bent down to talk to Meredith, who went all smiles when she saw him. "How's my little punkin?" he asked.

Tip watched them, absorbed. She wished she had the right to reach down and ruffle Rob's dark hair, the way she had been ruffling his daughter's red fuzz all day. Then she remembered why she had come over. "Have you looked at my car?"

Rob straightened up. "Yep."

"It's all fixed?"

"Nope."

"Oh. I just thought, I mean, it's getting late and all ..." Tip's voice trailed off.

"Maybe we'd better go into the office, Tip."

"Uh-oh. This is not sounding good." But Tip followed him into the office, where he parked Meredith next to the desk.

Tip promptly turned the stroller around to face the other way.

Rob looked at her questioningly.

"No reason for this sweet angel to have to look at that," she said, waving her hand at the calendar.

"That calendar really bothers you, doesn't it?" Rob said. Fred had hung it up there in the beginning of the year, and Rob hadn't objected, because generally only the three of them used the office. It wasn't as if Rob minded looking at pictures of naked women, but he barely noticed it was there now. He could see where a woman might object to it, though.

Tip didn't want to talk about the calendar. "What really bothers me is that my car isn't fixed. Are you going to tell me what's wrong?"

"I'm not exactly sure yet."

"You couldn't find what was wrong?"

"It's going to take a teardown to find the trouble," he said.

"Is that as major as it sounds?"

He nodded.

"Time-wise or money-wise?"

"Both."

"Wow." Tip had counted on her car being drivable today. She took a minute to process this new information. "Let me see if I have this right. You do a teardown, which costs money, to find out what is wrong, which will cost more money to fix."

"I'm afraid that's right."

"How much money are we talking here?"

"I can give you a teardown estimate, but I can't give you a repair estimate until I get in there for a look."

Tip bit her lip. "Can you at least give me an idea?"

Rob looked right at her. "Promise you won't go ballistic on me?"

"Yes. I really need to know."

He named a range that he thought was safe, and Tip went off like a rocket.

"*What!*"

At that, Meredith burst into tears and Ned burst into the office.

"Geez, Tip, you *promised*," Rob said. He picked up the baby and spoke soothingly to her.

"What happened?" Ned asked, unclenching his fists. Tip sank onto one of the chairs.

Rob answered him. "Tip wanted me to ballpark her repair."

"Oh." He looked shyly at Tip. "Cars are great when they're running, but when they're not . . ."

"Tell me about it," Tip murmured.

"Lucky you're a college professor instead of a working stiff like me," Ned said, with a tentative smile. "Why don't you just get rid of the car and buy a new one?"

"Because I might just as well walk on the moon," Tip said, exasperated. Then she lowered her voice. "I'm broke, all right?"

"Broke?" Rob echoed.

"Happens to everyone, sometime," Ned said sympathetically. "I hear those college loans are a bear to pay back."

"You hear right," Tip said. She turned to Rob. "Do you think I could get anything for the hunk of junk?" she asked him.

"Not much if you want to sell it as is," he answered honestly. "I'm not saying it's not worth fixing."

"I know. It will just take time, and money."

"If it will make it any easier, I'll give you what the scrap yard would give you for it, right now."

Tip thought for a moment. "Would you? That would save time."

Rob put Meredith back in the stroller, went over to his desk and pulled out a check ledger. He took his time, aware that after he gave Tip this check, she would be gone for good. "What will you do now?" he asked her.

"I'll call Mary Kate to come and get me. I guess I'll be staying with her for a while." Longer than she wanted to, now. Tip looked at Rob. "I appreciate your letting me stay with you last night. I was really stuck."

"No problem. Thanks for watching my baby for me."

"It was a pleasure. I know that sounds trite, but it's true. Meredith is a treasure."

Tip caught the baby's eye, and Meredith gave her a smile that tugged at the corner of her heart. "What will you do about Meredith?" she asked Rob.

He shrugged. "We'll get by until I find a new sitter. What will you do without a car?"

She managed a weak smile. "I'll get by too."

"Here," he said, handing her the check.

She took it, and for a moment they stood holding that same piece of paper. The moment stretched, their eyes locked, and Tip was overwhelmed by a sudden feeling of connectedness. Finally, Rob let go.

"Well, good luck," he said, unsmiling.

"You too." She was still held by his gaze, and he didn't seem to want to look away any more than she did. "I guess I should be going now," she said. It was time to leave, and leaving was what she did best, but oddly enough, Tip found herself fishing for an excuse to stay. Wishing Rob would ask her to.

"Shee-oot," came a voice from the doorway.

Rob and Tip looked over in surprise, both having forgotten that Ned was there.

"You two are no better off than you were this time yesterday, one with no car and one with no babysitter," he said.

Rob was looking at him as if the door itself had spoken.

Tip gave him a crooked little smile. "He's right," she said to Rob.

"And I want a say in this because I'm one of the ones who's going to be working my butt off if you don't have a babysitter, Rob. We're up to our elbows in cars here."

"I'll pay you and Fred overtime, like before."

"It's not the money," Ned said with a snort of disgust. "I've got a life, you know."

Tip wondered what he would spend more time on—watching baseball, playing video games or tractor racing—but she held that thought.

"Fine," Rob said. "Have your say."

Ned suddenly turned shy again, now that he had their full attention. Tip looked at him politely and waited. Rob stood with his arms crossed over his chest. "You both know as well as I do," Ned said, taking off his baseball cap, scrunching it around in his hands and then plopping it back onto his head. "The deal was your idea in the first place."

"My watching Meredith today while Rob looked at my car?" Tip said.

"It worked, didn't it?" Ned said.

Tip nodded. Ned looked at Rob.

"Yeah," Rob said guardedly. "What's your point?"

Ned shook his head. "I know I'm not the brightest guy in Madison, but you two— Don't you get it? I mean, if it worked for one day..." he said with a shrug, and with that headed back out to the garage, leaving Rob and Tip staring after him.

Tip mused, "He means that I should stay and babysit Meredith—"

"While I fix your car," Rob finished.

They stood there in silence. Tip told herself she needed a working car, and she sure wasn't going to be able to buy one with the check she held in her hand. She needed a place to stay while she looked for a job, and she sure wasn't going to be able to pay for that for very long either. The idea made perfect financial sense. She could watch Meredith and still look for a teaching job for fall, have a roof over her head in the meantime and drive away in her own car.

Rob seemed to be going through a similar thought process.

"What do you think?" she said finally.

"That there's no way you're going to go for it."

She was taken aback. "Why do you say that?"

"You're a college professor."

"Instructor."

"Whatever. Watching my baby for a day when you literally had no alternative was one thing."

Tip couldn't help bristling. "So you think I'm some kind of academic snob, or something? That I think taking part in the day-to-day growth of a developing human being would be beneath me?"

"That's a fancy way to describe a job that entails a lot of wiping up after what comes out of both ends of said human being."

"You've had Meredith for four months, Rob Winfield," Tip said hotly. "Don't pretend you don't know how rewarding time with her is."

He stared at her. "Are you telling me you're interested in this?"

She crossed her arms. "I like Meredith, I need my car, I'm out of money... What do you think?"

"All right, I'll take your word for it. As far as I'm concerned, if you will mind her as long as it takes me to get your car back on the road, we can call it even."

Tip bit her lip. She could only do this if she could continue to stay in his house, but she could hardly ask to do that.

He read her silence with uncanny accuracy. "Room and board included," he added softly. "What do you say?"

Tip didn't stop to analyze the fluttery feeling that had taken up residence in her middle during the last twenty-four hours. She didn't even pretend to herself to weigh the pros and cons.

"Let's do it," she said, handing the check back to him. Then she got behind the stroller. "Now for my end of the bargain. Meredith and I will see you at supper."

Rob watched them go, absently tearing up the check in his hand and wondering whether Ned was due for a raise.

He was glad Tip wouldn't be leaving today. Having her around would make life a lot easier for him.

Except on one very basic level. It was going to be hard to keep his hands off her. He was definitely at the point in his attraction to her where he would typically switch to the hands-on approach with a woman. But things were different with this woman. It was hands-off, hands down.

He groaned and went back out into the garage to put his mind to figuring out how her car was put together.

Too bad his mind was firmly fixed on how Tip was put together.

The next morning, Rob had already fed Meredith and was playing with her on his lap when Tip wandered into the kitchen.

Rubbing her eyes the way Meredith did when she was sleepy, Tip made her way unerringly to the coffee and filled a mug.

"Hi," she said in a froggy voice, depositing the mug on the table and shuffling out the door to the porch. A few minutes later she reappeared, with a newspaper in her hand, and dropped into a chair.

"Where did that come from?" Rob asked.

"From the paper girl. I met her yesterday afternoon when she was riding her bike past and told her to start delivery today," said Tip, already immersed in reading.

Rob smiled and turned his attention back to Meredith. He supported her under the arms while she stood bouncing on his lap, bending and straightening her knees. It was one of her favorite games.

"Hey, Tip," he said. "Look how strong she is. I'll bet she'll be walking soon."

Tip threw him a doubtful look over her paper. "I don't think most babies walk until they're about a year old."

Rob snorted. "Did you hear that, Meredith? Tip thinks you're like most babies."

Tip rolled her eyes and went back to reading. Rob watched her, knowing he was far gone if he couldn't keep his eyes off of her when she looked like that. Her hair was in its typical morning muss, the oversized T-shirt she wore over faded jeans concealed even more of her figure than the baggy sweats had yesterday morning, and she had a crease from the pillowcase running diagonally across her cheek. She yawned, opening her mouth so hugely that her hand couldn't cover it all. Overall she was not exactly your classic image of feminine allure.

But Rob found himself wanting to do things with her that would make her hair straighten. Thinking of such things was not the wisest thing for a man who had an exuberant baby tromping around on his lap to do, so he focused again on Meredith, lifting her up over his head, then lowering her down for a kiss. Up, down, kiss. Up, down, kiss. This was another of her favorite games, and it set Meredith to giggling.

Rob saw out of the corner of his eye that Tip was watching them, but when he looked at her, she dropped her eyes back to the paper. Finally she folded it up and offered it to him.

He shook his head.

She shrugged and pushed back her chair, stretching. "I think Meredith and I are going to pound the pavement again this morning."

"Will you need a car?"

Tip thought about that. "Maybe later," she said. "Since I'm going to be here for a little while, it's probably a good idea for me to know my way around. Do you need any groceries or anything?"

"There's always a list there," he said, pointing to the refrigerator. "Nothing that can't wait until I go on Saturday, but if you're out anyway..."

"No problem."

"If it's all right with you, I think I'll get over to work a little earlier this morning. Here are the keys to the Jeep that's in the driveway." He held them out.

Tip took them from him, and felt a thrill sizzle up her arm when her hand touched his. It was like play-acting in a cozy domestic scene. The wife and baby seeing off the father for a day of work. The part of the wife was being played by Theresa Irene Padderson.

"Well, have a good day," she finally said. "Don't worry about us. We'll be just fine."

"I know you will."

Like good fathers everywhere, Rob leaned down to kiss his baby goodbye before he went to work. But of course, he didn't kiss the babysitter.

Tip and Meredith set out on their stroll right away, and got to the variety a little earlier than before. This morning, the tiny store was crowded. Tip picked up a Providence newspaper and stood in line, noticing that Ned was in position at the video game. She also noticed that today his concentration seemed to be suffering because of the frequent, surreptitious looks he gave to a petite blond woman who was working behind the combination deli-bakery counter at the back of the store.

Tip was still smiling to herself when it was her turn to pay. The woman from yesterday was working the front register. "Hello again," she said, over the background noise in the store. "Number today?"

"No, thanks," Tip said. That could quickly become a habit, and she didn't have much money to spare.

"She sure is a cutie," the woman said, looking at Meredith. "She's got your hair."

Now that she was going to be living in town for a while, Tip wanted to set the record straight. "She's not mine," she said. "I'm her babysitter."

"Oh?" The woman handed Tip her change, her tone idly curious. "Whose is she?"

"Her father is Rob Winfield."

The background noise died noticeably. It seemed to Tip that all ears in the store were tuning in as the woman repeated, "Rob Winfield? Well she sure is a cute little thing. Not that anyone in town expected anything less, when news got out that the two of them were having a baby. Turned out to be a strange situation, though, didn't it?"

Eerily, Tip felt more than saw all eyes turn to her as she tried to think of a reply. Before she could, another voice cut in.

It was Ned. "Hey, Tip," he said easily, without a trace of his customary nervousness. "Ready to go?"

Tip managed a little wave to the woman behind the counter before Ned ushered her out. When she glanced back and saw the crowd staring after them, open-mouthed, she guessed that Ned had just created as much gossip as he'd set out to stop.

When they got out the door, he dropped his hand from her elbow and started to turn red, as if he just realized what he'd done.

Tip followed him over to his pickup truck, which was parked in the far corner of the lot. "What in the world was that all about?" she said.

Ned cleared his throat. "I have an idea Rob hasn't brought you up to speed on Meredith's mother."

"You're right about that."

"Now that you're going to be staying here for a while, he ought to. Those gossips in there would have done the job for him if they'd realized you were in the dark. They live for a chance like that."

"No doubt." Tip remembered what Rob had said about how news traveled in this small town. She waited, watching Ned struggle with what to say next.

"Shee-oot. I guess you're better off hearing it from me," he finally said. "Her name is Sondra. She was a waitress when Rob started dating her a few years ago." He paused, and added, "They weren't married."

"Did they have any plans for the future?"

Ned gave a nervous laugh. "Marriage plans? Not as far as I could see, and I saw more than most. Sondra was a looker, but not the settling-down type. She was hell-bent on becoming a professional model. And at that time, marriage was about the farthest thing from Rob's mind. You could say that what they had was...convenient."

Tip thought about how drastically Rob's life must have changed, since Meredith had come along.

"Of course, after Sondra told him she was pregnant, Rob asked her to marry him," Ned added quickly. "But she didn't want to. Didn't even want to have the baby."

"What?" Tip's voice was almost a whisper.

Ned nodded. "You heard right. Rob went through hell and back, talking her into it. Never saw him so tore up about anything." He shook his head, then went on. "Funny thing was, after Sondra started to show, she got her break modeling. The agency she was hooked up with wanted pregnant women.''

Tip cleared her throat. "What happened when Meredith was born?''

He shrugged. "Motherhood didn't change Sondra. Modeling was still the most important thing in her life. She made tracks out of Madison the minute she could. Story goes that she got her figure back fast, and now she's in New York modeling, uh—'' He paused, his face reddening. He looked at Tip, then looked away. Finally he gave up and got into his truck.

Tip just watched, mystified, as he turned on the engine and started to pull away. She was even more surprised when he put on the brakes and backed up next to her again.

"Underwear,'' he said.

"I beg your pardon?''

"Sondra. She models...fancy underwear and such.'' Even his ears were red as he drove away.

After he left, Tip stood there in the parking lot, cherishing the feel of Rob's precious baby in her arms, for a long, long time.

Work at the garage continued to back up, so Rob called Tip at lunchtime to tell her he couldn't get away. He could hear Meredith screeching in the background.

"What's she doing?'' he asked.

"Her squeaky-gate imitation,'' Tip said cheerfully. "Don't worry. Everything's fine. We'll see you later.''

Later, she didn't sound so cheery. She met Rob at the back door holding a squalling, red-faced Meredith out at arm's length. "Here,'' she said, thrusting the baby into his hands. "Wet, fussy, drooling . . . yours."

Rob cradled his daughter against his chest. Tip was picking up her shoulder bag and sunglasses from the kitchen table. "Bad afternoon?" he asked.

She glared at him. "It was the afternoon from hell, if you must know. She's chewing on everything in sight and drooling buckets. She wouldn't play anything, wouldn't take her nap, and fussed on low volume for three hours, except for the times she was fussing on high volume. The poor child was miserable, and the worst part was, I couldn't do a darn thing about it." She headed for the door.

"She must be—wait! Where are you going?" Rob was a little worried. She wasn't leaving *already,* was she? As happy a baby as Meredith was, there were bound to be days like this. Was Tip going to go back on their deal at the first sign of trouble?

"I'm going to do something about it," Tip said. "The bulletin board at the variety said there was a babysitting class beginning tonight at the rec center. It starts in five minutes and I intend to get a front-row seat."

Rob smiled as he rocked back and forth with Meredith, whose squalling had dulled to a whimper. "Isn't that a class for young girls who want to learn how to babysit?"

Tip must have glared at him again, but it was hard to tell now that she had her sunglasses on.

"I don't care if it's for migrating waterfowl. If it can tell me what to do to help her, I'm going." She slammed out the door.

"Take the Jeep!" Rob yelled after her, but she was already starting the engine. He let out a sigh of relief that ended in laughter. Tip intended to stay, all right, and what's more, she was going to single-handedly battle the evils of teething. He wiped Meredith's drippy chin and watched his car disappear down the road.

Meredith was asleep—finally—when Tip came back. Rob handed her the beer he had just opened and got another for himself. He popped the top and took a swig.

"Rough evening?" she asked, pouring hers into a glass.

She was smiling now, he noticed. "We've had better," he admitted. "How was class?"

"Great! I'm so glad I went."

"You mean you found out something that will help with her teething?"

"You knew she was teething? Why didn't you say something?"

He was about to answer that he hadn't been able to get a word in edgewise, when she went on.

"We have to make sure to give her lots of things that are safe for her to chew on. There's not much else we can do except wait for the tooth to come in."

"It was worth sitting there for three hours, to find that out?"

Tip's eyes were shining. "That's not all I learned," she said excitedly. "And there are two more classes, the next two nights. Don't you just love the power of education?" She frowned. "It *is* all right if I go out at night, isn't it?"

Rob chuckled. "Of course. I just need you to look after Meredith during my working hours."

"I can watch her at night, too, when you go out," Tip offered, taking a step toward him.

The muscles of his jaw tightened, then relaxed again. "No need."

"Really, it's all right. I'd be here anyway," she reasoned, unconsciously taking another step in his direction. "Let's face it, I'm kind of stuck here, with no car and not knowing anyone."

"I never go out at night," he said with finality, his eyes locked on hers.

"Oh." Tip felt her heartbeat gain momentum. It must be her imagination, but it seemed that in the space of a few moments, the atmosphere in the room had become fully charged, crackling with possibilities.

He leaned toward her. "So be warned," he said, his lips curved in a faint smile that didn't reach his eyes. "Since you're stuck here, you're stuck with me."

She registered the intensity in his blue eyes, suddenly aware of how close he was—and of how, on some unknown level, she wanted him even closer.

Neither trusting the desire she felt in him, nor understanding her own, she forced a little laugh and stepped around him to the sink. "I can handle that," she said lightly.

"Can you, Tip?"

She turned and looked him straight in the eye then, and Rob felt his insides bottom out.

"I can handle *anything*," she said.

Rob watched the outline of her behind under her long tunic top as she walked down his hall and into his spare room.

If she could handle anything, he wondered, why did she seem to be running away from something?

Chapter Five

It wasn't quite true, what she had told Rob the night before. She *used* to be able to handle anything, Tip conceded. Growing up, she had done well in school and in sports and was close to her family and friends.

Physically, she had been a late bloomer. But by the time she entered college, she had developed a figure that coincided with the popular male notion of the ideal female. A centerfold figure. The stares and the comments that came her way were bad enough. But worse, guys now wanted to date her for her body, not her company.

She tried her best to handle it. She could ignore the stares; and the comments, she could combat with a quick retort. But she couldn't make a man—especially a college man—notice her nonphysical attributes. It seemed that their universally held belief was that a woman with a body like Tip's had to be a loose woman.

She had never particularly considered herself a prude, but in the end, it was easier simply to become one. So she stopped dating and concentrated on her studies. She progressed quickly, and the further along she went, the more she found that the academic world brought her into contact with men who could appreciate, if not all of the qualities that made her who she was, at least her intellect.

None more so than the professor who was her mentor and friend in her graduate program. Michael Tarlington was fifteen years older than she, divorced, and so refreshingly different from other men that Tip let her guard down with him. He was handsome and charming and treated her with forbearance and respect. So it was little wonder that, at the age of twenty-one, she found herself married to him.

She had gotten her first teaching job right there, in the same department as Michael, and they had a circle of friends on the campus. She was thrilled with the match, and was convinced that her new husband looked on it as she did, as a meeting of the minds, a union on a lofty plane. Besides, he was surely too old to be very interested in what men her own age seemed to regard as the be-all and end-all of existence.

But a solely intellectual merger was not Michael's design, she soon found out. He might not have seemed interested in her body before they were married, but that changed drastically. Tip had not been naive enough to think that they would never have a physical relationship; and after all, she loved children and badly wanted some of her own. The trouble was, Michael seemed preoccupied with sex.

Before long, he became frustrated with her lack of interest and confronted her.

"What's wrong? I thought all that modesty and prudishness before we were married was because of your old-fashioned values. You're my wife now. You don't have to hold back."

She wasn't holding back. In fact, she *tried* to make herself respond to him. But without success. *Was* something wrong with her? It was mortifying to have her husband find her lacking as a woman. And he didn't hide his growing disappointment.

"Why is sex so important, anyway?" she had finally asked. "That's not why you married me." Although lately she wasn't so sure. Michael had made a flippant comment about her performance not measuring up to her equipment. He'd apologized for it, but it still bothered her. She wondered how much truth was behind it.

"Maybe not, but sex *is* important in a marriage," he had countered. "Remember, I've had more experience than you. Keep trying. It's bound to work."

She did; it didn't.

Finally, Michael told her he thought they should go for counseling. Sex therapy.

She refused. He insisted. She left.

So the marriage that Tip had had such high hopes for had blown up in her face. And so had her career, because she wanted off that campus at any cost. Away from Michael and all of their friends, whose apparent knowledge of the details of her marital inadequacies only added to the pain of her failure. Since then, she had kept moving, and kept to herself.

Until now.

Now, when she suddenly found herself knee-deep in the day-to-day life of one Rob Winfield. Not only falling prey to the charms of his baby daughter with each hour she spent caring for her, but also living in the same house with a man who made her feel things she had never felt before. She was very aware of her growing attraction to him, and the wonder of it all was, it was a physical attraction.

No doubt about it, to be attracted to a man like Rob was asking for exactly the kind of trouble that was hard for Tip to handle.

I can handle it, she told herself as she assembled peanut butter and jelly sandwiches for their lunch. It was a food that was difficult to eat with any degree of attractiveness. A simple cure for what had to be no more than a simple case of the hots.

"How has she been this morning?" Rob asked when he came in from work.

Meredith, who was sitting in her swing, beamed at him. "Better than yesterday," Tip said. "She's still happiest when I can keep her distracted. I had her in the stroller most of the morning, walking the streets of Madison."

Rob ate peanut butter sandwiches without a complaint. And Tip had been wrong. He looked sexy as the dickens, with the muscles in his clean-shaven jaw working to chew the sticky stuff. When Tip realized she was watching in fascination, she quickly hoisted her own sandwich and deliberately took a bite that was large enough to keep her occupied for a while.

"I was wondering," he said suddenly.

She was still chewing. "Mmm?"

"Do you have a bathing suit?"

Tip choked on the milk she was drinking to wash down her sandwich. Rob stood up and put a hand on her shoulder while she coughed uncontrollably.

"Are you all right?" he asked when she finally stopped.

Tip was very conscious of his hand on her shoulder. She nodded, wiping her eyes, then watched as he got Meredith out of the swing and settled her in his lap for a bottle.

"Do you?" he finally said.

"Why do you want to know?" she asked stiffly.

He looked at her, puzzled. "I'm going to open the pool this weekend, and I thought if you didn't have a suit with you, you might want to pick one up while you and Meredith are out."

"Oh." Tip relaxed, but only slightly. His intentions may be honorable, but the last thing she needed was for any man, especially a man like Rob Winfield, to see her in a bathing suit. "Thanks, but I don't swim."

"You don't swim?"

"Why are you looking at me like that? Not everyone swims."

"We can fix that. I'll teach you," he offered.

"I said I don't swim!" Too late, Tip realized how sharp her voice sounded.

Rob looked even more puzzled. "Fine," he said. "But you may want to get a suit anyway. The shallow end is big, and you may want to take Meredith in. I'll buy some floaty things for her. I thought it would be something for the two of you to do during the day, since the weather has turned hot."

Tip decided to change the subject. "I wanted to look something up this morning, but I couldn't find any books on baby care."

Rob finished burping Meredith. "Baby care?"

"You know, those reference books on health, safety, nutrition. That sort of thing. Our teacher was telling us about them in class. You do have one, don't you?"

"No."

Tip was surprised. "How did you learn so much about babies?"

"Through osmosis," he muttered. He cleared his throat. "Actually, Meredith has a very good pediatrician, and I pay close attention to everything she tells me."

Tip got the shopping list from the refrigerator. "You may not need a book about babies, but I do," she said, adding it to the bottom of the list.

Rob stood up and gave her that crooked grin that made her insides jumble up. "Write bathing suit, too," he said, and went out the door for work.

Tip watched him cross the lawn. "In your dreams," she said softly.

Tip had the dream again, that afternoon when she dozed off over the paper while Meredith napped. In the dream she was naked, and bright lights shone on her. Beyond them, in the dark, were men. Lots of men. She couldn't see them, but she could hear their voices, and knew they were all looking at her. She had to run; but she couldn't move. She was pinned down by beams of hot light, agonizingly on display, screaming for someone to help her get away. But no one did. No one ever did.

She woke up suddenly, drenched in sweat, her heart pounding. Meredith was crying in her crib. Grateful for being pulled back to the here and now, Tip went to her. Fleetingly, she wondered if Rob had been part of her dream audience this time.

Later on, she took Meredith to the garage. Fred saw them first. "Change your mind about going out with me, doll?" he asked smoothly.

"No, thank you," she said sweetly.

"I guess you really are Rob's exclusive property," he said with a wicked grin.

Tip stiffened. "You know what our deal is, Fred."

"Yeah. I know what they're saying up at the variety, too, now that folks have gotten a gander at you, doll. Course, the way Ned left with you yesterday morning, talk is that the three of us are sharing you. All I want is my fair share," he added with mock innocence.

Tip was wondering how hard she'd have to hit him to render him unconscious, when Ned appeared from behind a truck.

"Shut *up*, Fred," he said, and then steered Tip away. "Don't let the gossip get under your skin, Tip." He handed her a bulging paper sack. "Here. This is for you," he said, turning red, and turning on his heels.

Tip peered into the sack at a jumble of pink stalks with green leaves. Rob walked up behind her and looked over her shoulder. "Mmm. Rhubarb," he murmured in her ear.

His warm breath gave Tip a warm shiver. "You eat this?"

"Nothing like homemade rhubarb pie."

Tip called across the garage, "Thank you, Ned. But I think you should know that I can't bake my way out of a paper bag."

Rob was tickling Meredith. "I just got a call that my class has been moved up an hour tonight," Tip told him.

"I can be home early," he said, before she even had a chance to ask him.

"I appreciate it," she said. "Especially knowing how busy you are."

"The class is making you a better sitter, which is good for my daughter. Nothing is more important than that."

Tip felt her throat swell with emotion. She was not a sap. It was just that he was such a caring father.

"Besides," he added with a mischievous smile, "I'll take it out of the time I was going to spend on your car.

All right. So maybe she was a sap. And an even bigger one when she strolled Meredith up to the variety and handed the bag of rhubarb to the object of Ned's longing glances.

"Is it really possible to make this into a pie?"

The young woman, who Tip had found out was named Susie, smiled shyly and nodded, her silky blond hair falling back neatly into place. "This will make two."

"Great. I'll pay for them now." After a pause she added, "It's from Ned's garden."

Susie's eyes lit up, and then her smile faded.

Tip leaned in over the counter and lowered her voice. "Have you heard the rumors about Ned and me?"

The girl nodded.

"Well, the truth is that I think Ned is a great guy, but he's not interested in me. He has his sights set on someone else. Have you noticed?"

Susie colored and looked down.

"I'll pick up one of the pies tonight," Tip said. "The other, I'd like you to hand deliver to Ned next time he comes in. All right?"

Looking up, Susie nodded. Her eyes, Tip noticed, were lit up again.

As Tip drove home from babysitting class that evening, she paused in wonder at having thought of Rob's house as "home." She had never done that before, in all the places she had lived over the years.

She shook her head, and put it down to some kind of nesting instinct that had been awakened along with the maternal ones that seemed to appear daily as she cared for Meredith.

Then there was the pie instinct, she thought, staring glumly at the white box she had picked up at the variety on the way home. That one had to do with Rob's humming "mmm" into her ear at the garage, and her thinking that he needed a treat. He never complained, but he never seemed to go out and do anything for himself. When he was home, he was with Meredith whenever she was awake. And he had to be tired from getting up with her during the night.

Tip woke up too, now. She hadn't the first night, but since then she found that the tiniest cry in the dark had her sitting bolt upright in bed, on full alert. She'd listen as Rob went to Meredith, his voice soothingly low, sometimes singing. And when she heard his footsteps going back to his own room, she relaxed and went to sleep.

Usually not right away, though. It was hard to sleep, when she thought of him lying there on the other side of the wall. In her less guarded moments she found herself wondering what it would be like if he came to her room one night, instead of his own.

Which was why she stayed on guard.

Pulling in the driveway, she saw that the light in Meredith's room was on, which meant that she wasn't asleep yet. Tip went up the back stairs quietly. She paused in the kitchen. The television was on, and in the glow from its screen Rob lay on his back on the sofa, eyes closed. Meredith lay on him, tummy to tummy, looking relaxed as only a sleeping baby can look. He stroked her back, softly and rhythmically.

When the commercial ended, Tip heard her favorite quiz show host ask a question. Then Rob softly murmured the answer. She drank in the scene, listening in fascination. He never opened his eyes, but no matter what the category, Rob responded before the contestants, and he was right more often than not. Tip smiled. She may teach on the college level, but the breadth of Rob's knowledge put her to shame. A mechanic? Apparently by choice.

Feeling guilty about eavesdropping, Tip started rustling around in the kitchen. Rob appeared in the doorway with Meredith, still sleeping, on his shoulder. "I didn't hear you come in," he said.

"I was being quiet. I didn't want to wake her. You know, I was talking to the class instructor, and reading through some literature, and I am beginning to think that Meredith might have a cold."

"Not might. Does."

"How do you know?" she asked in wonder.

He shrugged. "Her nose is running and she's all stuffy."

"What do we do?"

"Don't worry, Tip. Kids get colds all the time. I have the humidifier running in her room. She's uncomfortable, but she can still do all her normal activities. Just like you would if you had a cold."

"I feel guilty," Tip confessed. "She probably got it from coming out with you in the rain when my car broke down."

"Old wives' tale. You can't get a cold from being cold or damp. You get a cold from a virus. Just relax, Tip. She'll be fine." He looked at the counter. "What did you get?"

Tip cut the string and opened the white box to show him.

Her heart leaped when he flashed his blue eyes at her, smiling. "Well I'll be," he said. "I'm going to put her down now. Feel like making some coffee to go with that?"

"Sure." Tip leaned over his shoulder, where Meredith slept. Physically, she felt his presence more than she had ever felt another human being's, and close up, the feeling intensified. She kissed the baby on her soft, cool forehead. "Sleep well, little one," she whispered.

When Rob came back to the kitchen with the baby monitor, the coffee was ready and two slices of pie sat on plates on the counter. He picked them up, and said, "Let's go outside." Tip grabbed the coffee mugs and followed him through the porch and out to the deck in back.

They sat on chairs in the darkness, side by side, eating forkfuls of pie and listening to the crickets and the quiet static on the baby monitor.

When he finished his pie, Rob set the plate aside and cradled the coffee mug in both hands. "That was nice."

Tip swallowed the last of her pie. "It sure was. I never would have believed it, myself. Susie did a good job with that ugly-looking stuff, didn't she?"

Rob grinned. "Yeah, but I wasn't talking about the pie. I was talking about your getting it for me. It's been a long time since anyone has done something like that for me."

"Since Meredith's mother left?" Tip asked quietly.

After a moment, Rob gave a dry laugh. "Way before then. Thoughtfulness was not one of Sondra's strong suits," he said. "I'm surprised Ned didn't tell you that, too."

So he knew that she knew about Sondra. "You don't mind that he told me about Meredith's mother?"

"Mind?" Rob propped his feet up on the deck railing. "He gave *me* hell about leaving you in the dark. Said you had a right to know, now that you're going to be here for a while."

"You *do* mind."

"Hell no," he said irritably. "It saved me from having to tell you myself."

"He's kind of protective of me," Tip said apologetically.

"No kidding." Rob's voice was a low rumble in the darkness. "At least you got the real story from him."

Tip felt the instinct that had driven her to buy the pie make another assault on her. She wanted connection again, the kind she'd felt when they were both holding the check the other day, only more. She settled for resting her hand on his arm for a brief moment. His skin was warm, and she was aware of the masculinity of his arm in the hard muscle and crisp hair that she felt under her hand before she removed it. She swallowed, wondering if as big a fool as Sondra seemed to be actually walked the earth. "She gave you sole custody?"

"Yup."

"She doesn't want any role in Meredith's life?"

"Nope."

"What if she changes her mind?"

"My lawyer made it awful damn hard for her to do that. If she does, we'll butt heads over that bridge when we get to it."

Tip could see the determination in his profile, even in the dim light. As for her, she seethed at the thought of a woman who had had her own dearest dream, and had thrown it away so callously.

He must have sensed her emotion. "Hey, it's all right, Tip," he said. "All in all, things turned out for the best. It was better for her to leave sooner than later, for Meredith's sake."

"It will be hard for her, growing up without a mother."

"Better none than one like that," Rob said grimly.

"But she doesn't have to have one like that," Tip pointed out.

"I know," Rob said, rubbing the back of his neck. "Believe me, there's nothing I'd like more than to find a woman who could be a real mother to Meredith. But I'm going to be awfully choosy about it. She's going to have to be of strong character, and a stayer. No woman is going to leave my baby again," he said with fierce determination.

A stayer. Tip didn't hear what he said after that. All she heard was the echo of the slam of a door down one of the corridors of her mind. It was the door to her future. She would never be Meredith's mother. Or Rob's wife.

The thought shocked her. Where had it come from?

She hadn't realized until that moment that she wanted those things, until the thought had struck a chord on some deep, unknown level.

Tip struggled for some perspective. She really couldn't blame Rob for wanting the best for his daughter, even though she couldn't help being a little bitter that she herself wouldn't make the first cut. "So according to your standards, Meredith's own mother isn't good enough to be her mother," she said wryly.

"Don't get me wrong. I'm no prize," Rob said evenly. "But at least I stayed."

That, too, hit home. He hadn't left, but Tip left all the time, and she was leaving now. She stood up. "I know it really wasn't my business, but I feel better now that I know the story."

Rob felt better too, except about her getting up to leave. "Let's go in," he suggested. If he went in too, he could pretend she wasn't walking away from him, which was what was really happening.

"While we're on the subject," Tip said as they walked into the kitchen, "I forgot to give you your phone messages before."

Rob took the papers she handed him, leafed through them without interest, then dropped the whole bunch into the trash can.

Tip's eyes widened. "You mean you aren't going to call any of them back?"

"Nope."

"Most men would be flattered that women call to ask them out. Most men would say yes to one of them." There was going to be a dance at the rec center, and women had called throughout the day to ask Rob to go.

He blew out a gust of breath. "Do you know what they really want?" he said. "Not just a date to the dance. For some reason, the fact that I am a single father has suddenly made me prime husband material. I feel like a wanted man."

Tip was confused. "But you just said you wanted to find a mother for Meredith! I would think that a bunch of available women to choose from would be just what you're looking for," she argued.

Rob shrugged. It didn't make much sense to him either. Until now, he thought that all he wanted was a nice woman who would be a good mother to Meredith. But the woman who would be Meredith's mother would also be his *wife,* and suddenly, "nice" wasn't enough any more. The women who had left him those messages were nice—all of them. But they were also boring, blah, and absolutely colorless next to this woman with hair of flame and scintillating eyes, which looked like they could incinerate his kitchen and him with it right now.

And suddenly, something inside him caught fire. She was everything he wanted, and everything he couldn't have. But right at this moment, only the wanting mattered. He took her into his arms.

Resistance was the farthest thing from Tip's mind as he pulled her close. She lifted her face to his, mesmerized by the intense blue flame of his eyes. His breath warmed her lips for a tantalizing instant, and then his mouth came down to join with hers.

A sudden swift power flowed through the kiss. The intensity of the contact, lip to lip, breath to breath, shot through her like a lightning bolt, brilliant and unexpected.

And brief. They jolted apart, regarding each other warily.

Tip took a deep breath, letting her feelings slowly give way to her outraged intellect.

What had she been *thinking?* Mere moments before, on the deck, Rob had made it clear that he would never be serious about a woman like her. This kiss was nothing more than a physical whim. He was just like her ex-husband and all the other men she had known, and, worst of all, she had done her part to invite his advances. She couldn't, in all fairness, place sole blame on him for that kiss.

And, saints of heaven preserve her, *what* a kiss! She wouldn't be surprised if the ends of her hair were singed, the two of them had generated that much electricity. What she felt for him was far more powerful than she had imagined, and that made it scary. The best thing she could do was to make light of the whole thing.

She leaned back against the counter and crossed her arms. "Not bad, Winfield," she said, deliberately making her tone as casual as she could. "You ought to be able to conquer any eligible mother in town with that."

Rob had watched her struggling for control, not that he blamed her. He was doing a lot of that himself. That had been one hell of a kiss, and he knew damn well that she had felt it too. And although he wasn't fooled by her flippant attitude, he was one hundred percent in agreement that being casual about the whole thing was the best way to go. Being with a woman who was just making a brief stopover in his life, no matter how attractive she was, called for self-control, and he was just plain angry with himself for indulging his physical urge. As much as anything, that kiss had been an outlet for the frustration he felt over the barriers between them. But now that it was over, and had been so damn good, his super awareness of those barriers had only increased.

"I take it we're going to pretend that kiss never happened?" he asked offhandedly.

At great cost, she forced a smile. "What kiss?" she said lightly.

Tip hoped that would settle the matter, forever and always. She started to leave the room, but something made her stop and turn back again. "Would you mind if I gave you some advice?" she said, looking at him assessingly.

"Why do I have the feeling that you're going to give it to me whether or not I mind?" The corner of Rob's mouth twitched up.

Tip spoke seriously. "You might have to search far and wide to find a woman who meets your standards to be Meredith's mother. If you don't start returning some of those phone calls you get from women, you'll be father of the bride before you're a groom."

All the next day at work, Rob thought about what Tip had said. She was right that he had to start looking for a woman to be a mother to Meredith.

He glanced out of the office window at his house. Why not start looking right at home? Purely for argument's sake, of course.

There was no denying it. Even before that kiss, it was clear that something sparked up between him and Tip whenever they were together. It was partly physical, he knew. Rob figured he had already spent more time picturing her naked than all the other women in the world combined. But he also liked Tip, and respected her. That spoke to him.

Not only that, he was sure that she felt the same about him, despite the fact that most women in her position wouldn't be interested in a man who got his hands dirty on the job. Tip, he felt sure, didn't care about that.

She had a moral streak about a mile wide. He thought about the kiss again. Yes, there had been desire on her part, too, but it had been followed by a boatload of regret. He cursed, while vowing future restraint. He should have known. She was modest to a fault—even living in the same house with her, he'd never seen her less than fully covered up with those loose-fitting clothes she wore.

And she was old-fashioned about things like family. Cripes, she talked to her sister enough.

Most important of all, she had fallen for Meredith, hard. Rob could see it in the way she held his baby, spoke to her, tuned in to her. He hadn't known how gratifying it would be to share his baby with someone who thought she was as wonderful as he did.

But no matter how many points he found in Tip's favor, they didn't add up to a hill of beans against her rootlessness, the repeated pulling up stakes and moving on that characterized her past. In this all-important point, she was exactly like Sondra. It was the only thing he would never allow himself to take a gamble on.

He thought about Meredith's mother. Looking back, he knew that her leaving had been a relief. She had been destined to leave him and the baby. There was no stopping somebody who was on the run, whether they were running to something or away from something. It was clear to Rob that Sondra had been doing a little of both.

And Tip? What could she be running from, or to? Then again, there was always the possibility that she wasn't on the run at all. Maybe she just needed a reason to stay.

He wondered if he and Meredith might be reason enough.

As Rob climbed up the back stairs after work, he heard laughter coming from inside the house. He opened the kitchen door and found Tip and three young girls sitting around the table, which was littered with soda cans and pieces of paper. Meredith was looking at them, wide-eyed, from her swing in the corner of the room. Tip wiped a tear from the corner of her eye, she was laughing so hard.

One of the girls said, "Did you ever laugh so hard when you were drinking something that it came out your nose?" This prompted a new round of laughter.

"Who hasn't?" Rob said from the doorway, grinning. They all looked at him in surprise.

"Rob!" Tip said, smiling broadly. "Is it that time already?"

Laughter becomes you, he wanted to say. But of course, he couldn't, so he let his eyes tell her instead.

She looked away, flustered. "Rob, I'd like you to meet my classmates in the babysitting course. Girls, do you know Mr. Winfield?" she said, standing up.

LISA KAYE LAUREL   101

A bit self-consciously, the three of them stood up too. They regarded Rob curiously, no doubt measuring him against a twelve-year-old yardstick for male worth. He smiled at them, wondering how he measured up.

"I'm Jessie Grier," said the tallest of the group. She flashed him a shy smile. "My mother brings her car to you."

Carol Grier had gone to high school with Rob, and had had a baby the month after graduation. This was the baby. Rob liked Carol—he had been the first person she had seen when she walked out of the doctor's office after finding out she was pregnant, and he had lent her his seventeen-year-old shoulder to cry on. She had done a good job raising the kid, and all by herself, too.

The other two girls, Courtney and Jennifer, introduced themselves. He knew their parents, too. Tip had told him about meeting them all after class. He got Meredith out of her swing and greeted her with a hug and a kiss, then held her in his arms. "What are you doing?" he asked.

"Learning about babies," Jessie answered with a giggle.

"We have to take an exam tonight to pass the course," Tip explained. "No one had a brother or sister as young as Meredith to practice on, so I invited them over here."

"My daughter, the lab rat," Rob said with a grin. That brought a fresh round of giggling from the girls. Meredith opened her mouth wide and gnawed on his chin.

"Tip, are you going to let him get away with that?" Jennifer asked, hands on hips. "That baby is a little sweetheart and the farthest thing from a rat in the world!''

''Well, you know what they say—takes one to know one,'' Tip said dryly, sending the girls into a new round of giggles. She smiled at Rob. ''Meredith was great. She loved all the attention.''

''I can tell.'' Rob had noticed Meredith was turning her head curiously to look at each person talking. He started to clear a spot on the table to sit her in her infant seat.

''Hey, this isn't baby stuff,'' he said, looking at one of the papers in his hand. ''It's been a long time, but this looks like algebra.''

Tip was clearing the rest of the table. ''Oh, we were just doing a little math,'' she said lightly. ''We'd better get going, girls. Let me get my purse.'' She disappeared down the hall.

Rob looked at the girls. ''You do math for fun?''

Jessie wrinkled her nose. ''No way!''

''It was fun the way Tip did it, Jess! And I hate math,'' Courtney said.

''Me too,'' Jennifer agreed.

''Me too,'' Jessie said to Rob. ''I did so bad last year that I'm going to summer school for it. Tip was showing us a different way to do a problem. I wish she was my teacher.''

Tip walked back into the room then, dangling car keys in her hand. ''Who wants to drive Mr. Winfield's car?'' she asked the girls.

Rob felt his mouth drop, then close again when he saw Tip's grin.

''Don't you be late, now,'' he drawled, giving her his best sexy wink.

"And don't you get into any trouble while I'm gone," Tip shot back, smiling sweetly at him. Then she was swept out the door amid another chorus of giggles.

Watching her pile into his car with the girls and drive away, Rob laughed too.

He'd been doing a lot of that lately.

Chapter Six

Rob was up early the next day, getting some things he needed for the pool. He came back to the house later that morning with a sleeping Meredith draped in his arms. After settling the baby in her crib, he went into the kitchen, where Tip sat frowning over a portable typewriter.

"Grr." She yanked the paper out and wadded it into a ball. The ball sailed over toward Rob, who caught it with one hand.

Tip looked up from the keyboard, eyes wide. "I didn't know you were there," she said. "I was aiming for the trash can."

"Your aim was a little off." Rob sat down next to her. "I missed seeing you last night. Did you pass your exam?" He had been hoping she would sit out on the deck with him again in the dark. But he had crashed on the sofa before she came home, and she had gone to bed without waking him.

"Yes."

"Did Jessie and Jennifer and...who's the other one?"

"Courtney. Yes. All qualified babysitters you'll be able to use after I'm gone and you want to go out on dates," Tip pointed out.

Rob frowned. He didn't want to go on a damn date with anyone but her, and he didn't want to hear her talking about leaving. "What are you doing today?"

"Working on my résumé. What about you?"

"I'm going to open up the pool."

"Isn't it a little late in the summer for that?"

"It's been an unusual year," he reminded her. "I'm only opening it now because you're here."

Tip gaped at his brazenness. He was only doing this to see her in a bathing suit?

"I like to swim at night," he went on. "But even with the baby monitor, I wouldn't be able to hear Meredith if I'm swimming laps, or underwater. Now that you're here, I was hoping you wouldn't mind taking turns."

"Oh." Once again, Tip had misjudged him. Had she really become so suspicious over the last few years? "I'll be happy to listen for her while you're in the pool."

He leaned back in his chair and unwadded the piece of paper in his hand. "Could I take a look?"

Tip shrugged, then put a new piece of paper into the typewriter while he read.

He knew from what she had told him that first morning that she'd worked at five different colleges during the last five years. Talk about a rolling stone. But looking at it there in black and white he realized something else.

"Do you mind if I ask you something?"

"Why do I get the feeling you're going to ask me whether I mind or not?" she said.

She had him there. "Where have I heard that before?" he said, grinning.

"I can't imagine."

Rob rested an elbow on the table and half turned toward her. "Did you quit all these jobs, or were you canned?"

"I've never been fired," she said, with a little laugh. "Why would you think that?"

He studied her face. "Well, I'm not an academic, but I know what summa cum laude means. I can tell by the dates that you blew through college in three years, and were on the young side when you earned your master's. Very young. Your first teaching position was with a well-known university that is in the very first tier of selectivity."

"Your point?"

"If you weren't fired, why did you leave it?" The colleges she had taught at since then had been progressively less prestigious, which was not surprising, given her yearly departures.

"Rob, what *is* your point?" she asked, ready to duck any question whose answer centered around her divorce.

"Tip, this résumé doesn't make sense. You're clearly a superstar, ability-wise. But after an impressive start to your career, it's hardly taken a meteoric rise."

Tip sat in silence for several minutes. "Do you think it's easy out there in the academic world, Mr. Expert? Life on the tenure track is cutthroat at best, and let me tell you, everyone there is a superstar."

"Tenure track? Tip, you never stayed on the track long enough for the train to leave the station."

His insight stopped her in her tracks. She took a deep breath and said, "I've always been offered a contract renewal. I just never accepted it."

"Why not?"

Tip glared at him and grabbed the crumpled paper from the table in front of him. "All right, you've made your point," she said, and went back to her work.

Rob wanted to call her on not answering his last question. It was an essential part of her, this inconstancy. He wanted to get at the heart of it, so that he would know how to keep her from leaving. He softened his voice. "How do you explain your job-hopping to a potential employer?"

"I haven't had any trouble doing it the past four times," Tip said with a shrug. "I'll find a position somewhere."

That line of questioning was going nowhere. If she didn't want to talk about her past, it was none of his business, Rob reminded himself. But it was his guess that the reason she kept on the move had a lot to do with the shadows of pain that he sometimes saw in her eyes. "Isn't it awfully late to be looking for a position for this fall?" he said doubtfully.

"Yes, but I have a few things going for me. I'm a woman in a male-dominated discipline. I've got ability, sterling recommendations, and much more interest in a school's character than its prestige. I'd like to try working at a community college."

"What's your next step?" Rob asked.

"I'll have to see what's out there. That's why I'm polishing up my résumé. I'm going to a meeting in

Providence tonight, and I'm hoping to get some leads while I schmooze."

Rob looked at her. "Providence is not exactly just around the corner. How are you getting there?"

"I called around this morning and arranged for a taxi."

"That will cost an arm and a leg."

Tip gave him a half smile. "Just an arm," she said. "And it will be worth it."

"Saturday night is a funny time for a meeting. What group is it, anyway?"

"G.G.," she said, avoiding his eyes.

"What does that stand for?"

Tip cleared her throat. "Genuine Genius."

Rob looked at her through narrowed eyes. "Is that what it sounds like? One of those clubs for people who score a certain level on an IQ test or something?"

Tip looked down at the paper in her typewriter. "One of those."

All of a sudden he started laughing. "Well, that will sure be a wild time. Let the good times roll," he said, unable to resist teasing her. "I'll bet you intellectual types really trash a place, when you get going."

Tip sighed. "Are you finished yet? I've got to get working on this."

Still chuckling, Rob felt magnanimous. "Take the Jeep," he said.

"Oh, no, you don't have to—"

"Of course I don't. But take it anyway. I won't need it, and it will save you some bucks. Besides, I don't like the thought of you standing around some street corner in Providence tonight waiting for a cab."

Tip thought for a moment.

"Humor me," he urged.

"All right," she said finally. "I'll take it. Thanks."

"Take some advice too, and forget about community college. As far as teaching goes, I think there's somewhere else that you really belong. If you ask me—"

"I didn't."

He ignored her. "If you ask me—"

The phone rang. Rob leaned back in his chair and plucked the receiver from the wall behind him. "Hello."

The cheery voice on the line sang out, "Hi, Rob! How are you today?"

"Just fine, Mary Kate." It seemed to Rob that every time he answered his phone these days, it was Tip's sister.

"Have you got that pool open yet?" she asked.

"Not yet." He watched Tip as she crossed out and added words in pencil on her résumé, biting her lip in thought. Her lips looked luscious. He wouldn't mind doing a little nibbling there himself.

"…that G.G. meeting tonight. I sure hope she finds one."

Rob forced himself to pay attention to what Mary Kate was saying. "Me too," he said. "She sure could use one."

"It's just the place for someone like Tip to find one, too. Of course, the problem for her is staying with one."

"So I gathered. I was just telling her that all the good ones have probably been picked over by now."

"Don't tell her that, Rob!" Mary Kate objected. "That excuse has been around for centuries. We have to get Tip to think positive. One of these days she's

going to find the right one and settle down. Maybe
he'll be there tonight."

All at once Rob realized that he and Mary Kate were
talking about Tip finding completely different things
at that meeting. He covered the mouthpiece with his
hand and glared at Tip. "I thought you were going to
this meeting tonight to look for a *job,*" he said.

Tip looked surprised. "I am."

"Tell that to Mary Kate," Rob said, handing her the
phone. He grabbed the baby monitor and went outside to work on the pool.

Tip watched the screen door slam behind him,
wondering what he was being so touchy about all of a
sudden.

She stayed out of his way the rest of the day. By late
afternoon she had finished her résumé, showered, and
changed into a long, flowing top over a pair of slim
leggings. She walked out into the backyard, where Rob
was putting things away in the pool shed. Lying nearby
in her portable crib, Meredith smiled and started in on
a long string of chatter when she saw Tip.

Rob stopped what he was doing to take a long look
at Tip. She could almost feel him drinking her in. She
felt a blush start under his intense blue gaze, and tried
to think cool thoughts. Easier said than accom-
plished, with him standing there in nothing but a pair
of cutoff jeans, a sheen of sweat glistening over his
muscled upper body.

She bent down to wipe Meredith's nose, which was
still running from her cold. "How has she been today?"

"Not bad," he said. "She got fussy a time or two,
but overall she seems to be dealing with her cold pretty
well."

"Is it really all right if I go tonight?" Tip said with a worried frown. "I mean, if she's sick, maybe I'd better—"

"Go," Rob finished for her. "And find one. A job, I mean."

"That's what I'm looking for."

He stared at her, arms crossed over his bare chest.

Tip stared back at him. "Don't tell me this has to do with something my overly imaginative sister said on the phone."

"OK, I won't tell you."

Her eyes widened. "You think I'm going out on a . . . a manhunt?"

"It is a social meeting. And there will be men there—men you probably have a lot in common with."

"Unless one of them is holding a job offer in his hand, I'm not interested," Tip said with feeling. Then she paused, suddenly realizing something. "Anyway, what's it to you?" she challenged. "I'm your daughter's babysitter."

"What's it to me?" Rob started to go on, then restrained himself. He was being irrationally possessive. Where had this jealous streak come from? He had never felt this way about Sondra, or any other woman. Tip must think he had taken leave of his senses.

He decided to be honest with her. "Tip, whether you want to admit it or not, you are more to me than Meredith's babysitter. We're living in the same house, for cripes' sake." They were having intimate conversations. They had shared a kiss that had just about caused spontaneous combustion. And they were still exchanging smoldering gazes that, one of these times, they wouldn't be able to break off.

Completely misunderstanding, Tip looked at him in disbelief. "You're worried that I'm going to bring a man home with me?" she said hotly. "Let me assure you, Mr. Winfield, that I am not the kind that falls into bed with men at the least provocation. And even if I were, I would not be so crass as to entertain guests at a house where I am a guest myself. You have some nerve to imply that I have no more control over my sexual urges than . . . than *you* do."

All of a sudden, she stopped short, shocked that she had gone so far as to say that.

He stared at her, and Tip gained an appreciation for the concept of raw fury held under tight control. She edged toward the house. "I'm going to call a taxi."

"Why? You're taking the Jeep," he said curtly.

Tip started to protest, but he looked like he was in the mood to bend steel bars with his bare hands. "Take it and go," he said in a low voice.

"All right. I'm out of here," Tip said. "But I should warn you that my babysitting class instructor is going to be stopping by tonight." Although maybe *she* was the one who needed a warning, Tip thought.

"What the hell for?" he growled.

Good question, Tip realized. "She's the leader of a support group for single parents. I told her about you, and she said she had some information you might be interested in." Tip gave him a narrow glance. "She's also very nice and very single. At the time, I had the idea that you two might hit it off. I realize now, of course, how utterly ridiculous that was."

"Utterly," he echoed. "And that's the first thing you've been right about all day."

Without another word, Tip marched across the lawn, climbed into the Jeep and drove away.

* * *

If Tip was miserable on the drive to Providence, the drive home was worse. For one thing, Rob had been right about something, and Tip knew it. It was too late to be starting a job search for the upcoming academic year. She hadn't heard one piece of useful information about a position of any kind open in mathematics.

Even worse, she had met a man there. A nice man. Mary Kate would have salivated on his pricey Italian loafers, if she had been there. He had founded his own software company, and it had taken off like a rocket. And he hadn't bragged about it—Tip had found that out from someone else. He was handsome without being a pretty boy, polite without being a wimp, and interested in her without being pushy. What's more, he had enjoyed her company without once allowing his eyes to stray below her neckline.

Unlike Rob, whose fiery blue eyes had roamed all over her body with a look that had warmed her skin like the passion of a lover's touch.

"Rob!" Tip yelled at the interior of the Jeep as she sped along the highway in the dark. "I have just met a really nice man, so why am I thinking about Rob Winfield?"

She tried again to think of the software man. He was worlds more appealing than the other men she had met over the past few years, even the few she had dated. Dating disasters, all. This guy, though, didn't seem to be a body man. But then again, neither had her ex-husband. At first.

Rob Winfield was a body man, and he didn't try to hide it. Oh, he came with a few nice extras, like being a devoted father, a closet intellectual, and basically a nice guy. Tip couldn't deny that there was something at work between the two of them. He made her feel things, body and mind. What he felt about her was a little less complex and a lot more obvious. She didn't fit his image of a wife and mother, but he was clearly attracted to her physically. A body man, all the way.

But then there was the irritability he had shown today. After rethinking, Tip was unable to put it down to anything but jealousy. Odd.

Tip sighed. For better or worse, the software man, despite his promising future, was already history. The business card he had given her sat in the bottom of the trash barrel in a ladies' room back in Providence. A week ago, she'd have kept it, and maybe even gone out with him—once.

But that was then. Tonight, all she could think about was getting home to Rob and Meredith. Home. There it was again. She had to remind herself that it was *their* home, and she had no future in it. As soon as her car was ready, she would be leaving it, and them.

It was closing in on midnight when she pulled into the driveway. Rob had left the porch light on for her, but the rest of the house was dark, Tip noticed with relief. He must be asleep. She wasn't sure what kind of reception she would have gotten, considering the circumstances under which she had left.

But when she got inside, she found that he was still awake, and so was Meredith. He was in her room, rocking her to sleep in the glow of the night light, his muscular frame completely filling the rocking chair. Meredith snuffled and rubbed her eyes on his shoulder.

"Shh," he murmured, stroking the red curls on the back of her head. "It's all right, sweet girl. Daddy's here. Go back to sleep, angel."

"Hi," Tip said softly from the doorway. "Is everything all right?"

Rob looked up at her. "I think so, now. I had a hard time getting her to sleep before, and she just woke up warm."

"Warm?" Tip's voice rose. "You mean she has a *fever?*"

"Shh," Rob whispered again, but this time to Tip. "Everything's fine. It's just over one hundred. I gave her something to bring it down. She'll be fine once it kicks in."

He sounded so calm, especially for a new father. "How many times has she had a fever?" Tip asked.

"This is the first. Don't worry, Tip. It's not all that unusual." He paused. "How was your meeting? Did you get any job leads?"

All of a sudden, Tip felt desperately tired. "No. It was a total washout."

"I'm sorry," Rob said, sounding like he meant it. "I know you were counting on finding something soon." Meredith had stopped fidgeting and was settling down in his arms, but Rob kept rocking steadily. He looked like he could use some sleep himself.

Once again, Tip was seized by a compulsion to get closer to them, to embrace them both. She stood watching them, mesmerized, for what seemed like a long time. Then she whispered, "I had no right to say what I said earlier."

His voice came low and soft in the darkened room. "Forget it, Tip. I have."

Still, she stood there watching, absorbing the peace of the scene, far longer than she had an excuse to. At last, she roused herself to move away, to get herself into her own bedroom, nice and safe and alone.

"Sweet dreams, sweetheart," he murmured, his eyes half-closed.

Tip backed out of the room. Had his sleepy endearment been meant for Meredith, or for her?

There was no answer.

About an hour after Tip fell asleep, she was awakened by a cry in the darkness. Confused, disoriented, she bolted from her bed and ran into the hallway, where she collided with Rob.

"Are you all right?" Reflexively, he had wrapped his arms around her to keep her from falling, and he held her against him to steady her.

Tip was fully awake now. She knew where she was, she knew whose arms she was in, and she knew he was wearing nothing but shorts as well as she knew that she was wearing nothing but a long sleep-tee. Excruciatingly aware of her breasts pressed against his bare chest, she absorbed the heat of his body in the cool darkness of the hallway.

She nodded, her lips pressed against his shoulder. In that brief moment of entanglement, the crying had stopped, but suddenly it resumed in greater force. Rob's arms dropped and he ran into Meredith's room, with Tip right on his heels. He lifted the baby out of her crib while Tip turned on the light.

Meredith was wailing, her face red and scrunched up. "She's still warm," he said.

Tip put a hand to the baby's forehead. "Warm? Rob, she's burning up! Can you give her more—"

"No. Her last dose was less than two hours ago."

"Obviously it's not working, if she still has a fever."

He handed the baby to Tip. "That's not all. She's in pain. I think she has an ear infection. She needs to be looked at. Try giving her a bottle with water in it while I get a shirt and some shoes."

Meredith wasn't interested in the bottle. Tip tried to calm her, but she could feel the tension in every little muscle as the baby cried. When Rob came into the kitchen, diaper bag and keys in hand, Tip handed Meredith to him.

"I'm going with you," she said. There could be a long wait at a hospital emergency room in the middle of the night, and she wanted to be there to help.

Rob didn't argue. In the time it took him to strap Meredith into her car seat, Tip struggled into sweats and ran out the door.

"This is above and beyond the call of duty," he said as she buckled herself into the back seat next to the baby. "You could have gone back to bed."

Their eyes met in the rearview mirror. "No," Tip said. "I couldn't."

She spoke soothingly to the baby, not noticing much about the trip except that Rob was driving fast, but was calm and in total control. Long before she expected to reach the nearest hospital, which was several towns away, he stopped the car.

Tip looked up. They weren't at the hospital, or an all-night clinic, or even at Meredith's pediatrician's office in the next town. They were still in Madison, a few blocks behind Main Street, on a residential street Tip had become familiar with over the past week from strolling around with Meredith. The one with the big

Victorian houses, and shade trees whose branches arched and met over the street.

She didn't have time to ask Rob why they were stopping there. He had Meredith out of her seat and was halfway up a walkway to one of the houses before Tip caught up with him. He continued around to the back of the house, and handed the baby to Tip at the back door.

"Let's get her inside before we wake the whole neighborhood," he said, trying the doorknob. It was locked. Rob swore under his breath.

Tip felt more than a little confused. Meredith was whimpering against her shoulder, and Rob was counting the rocks that bordered a nearby flower bed. "What are you—" she began.

"Four, five," he said, and turned over a rock. He pulled out a key and went back to the door.

Tip gave up trying to figure out what he was doing. Obviously, he knew. She followed him in the door into a mudroom that opened onto a large kitchen. She couldn't see much, but Rob knew where he was going. He put an arm around her shoulder, guiding her from room to room until they came to the front stairs. Meredith started crying again.

A light snapped on in the stairwell. "What's going on down there?" a man's voice called out from the second floor.

"We've got a patient for you, Doc," Rob called back.

"Robby! What the devil's wrong?" Tip heard footsteps hurrying across an upper hallway. Rob turned on a light where they stood just as the man reached the bottom of the stairs, hastily belting his robe.

Tip's eyes widened. He wasn't smiling, and his salt-and-pepper hair was mussed from sleep, but there was no doubt about it. He was the man who had helped her when her car broke down, the Good Samaritan with the car phone.

He nodded briefly to her, all efficiency as he lifted the baby from her hands. "Well, well," he said, leading them into an examination room. "I was wondering when I was finally going to meet my granddaughter."

Tip followed them, lost in amazement. The doctor who was examining Meredith was Rob's *father*.

Slowly, things began to click into focus. It explained a lot of things, from their matching blue eyes, to the reason he knew Rob's home phone number, to Rob's curiosity when Tip told him she had run into him the next morning with Meredith.

And it left a lot of things unexplained. Like why Rob's father had never seen Meredith before now.

Meredith had protested being put on the table, so Rob was holding her while his father examined her. "Ear infection, all right. In full bloom," he said in a low voice. He looked in the baby's other ear. "This one is about ready to go, too."

"You never looked in her ears," Tip said to Rob, mystified. "How did you know that's what was wrong with her?"

He shrugged. "They're common with kids, especially with a cold. When she got fussy and spiked a fever, it was a logical guess."

"Especially for someone who grew up in a doctor's office," his father said in an aside to Tip. He gave Meredith a dose of antibiotics and gave Rob a prescription to fill at the pharmacy when it opened in the morning. While Rob gave Meredith a sponge bath to help bring her fever down, he spoke to Tip.

"It's about time we met properly. I am George Winfield, Rob's father."

Tip held out her hand. "I'm Tip Padderson, Dr. Winfield."

"That sounds awfully formal. Rob has always called me Doc, and you can too, if you like."

She smiled at him. "Once again, I'm witness to how well Winfield men handle an emergency."

"One of us is not too good on follow-up," he said, casting a glance at Rob. "I take it your car is still not running?"

Tip opened her mouth, then shut it again, reddening. She had been so involved with other things over the past couple of days that she hadn't even asked Rob about her car.

"We've worked out a deal, Doc," Rob said. "Tip is Meredith's live-in babysitter, while I work on her car."

"I know," his father said.

Rob frowned. "How?"

"Through the lightning-fast, far-reaching, more-reliable-than-not Madison grapevine." Doc paused, and added softly, "The same way I found out I was a grandfather."

He walked over to a cabinet and pulled out a fresh diaper, which he handed to Rob. He stood watching while Rob dressed the baby, then he took her in his arms. "Meredith," her grandfather said, gently touching his lips to her red baby fuzzhead. "Welcome to the family."

Tip felt the back of her throat sting as tears filled her eyes. It was a touching scene, and one that needed to be followed by a father-son chat. Which was a great cue for her exit, she thought, stepping toward the door.

Rob blocked her way. "Stay," he whispered in her ear. While she hesitated for a split second, he slung his arm around her shoulders to hold her in place next to him. As his father got acquainted with Meredith, Rob ran his hand lightly up and down the outside of Tip's arm.

Doc looked up at Rob. "You know that I have always had a soft spot for the babies in my practice. This little one is absolutely perfect in every way," he said. "You are doing a great job with her, Rob."

Tip felt tears brim up again.

"Thanks. That means a lot, coming from you," Rob said simply.

"I'm sorry things didn't work out with Sondra."

Rob's arm tightened around Tip. "All in all, Doc, I'm not. She wasn't cut out to be a mother."

"It couldn't have been easy for you, these past months."

"I'll grant you it's been a lot easier this past week, since Tip came along. I take it I have you to thank for that?"

"I only referred her as a customer."

His father handed the baby back to Rob. When he spoke again, Tip felt her heart shred.

"I could have helped you with the little one, Rob. I wanted to. When were you going to tell me?"

"I always call on your birthday, don't I?"

"Don't you think this warranted a special phone call?"

"Yeah. Something like, 'Hi, how about that game last night? By the way, I'm going to be a daddy.'" Rob's voice was sardonic. "I wonder what response I would have gotten to that?"

After a time, Doc sighed. "So do I, son," he admitted.

Neither seemed to know what to say after that. The silence stretched until finally Doc opened the door for them.

"I'm glad you brought Meredith here tonight. But you'd best be getting her home now. Remember, she'll need a follow-up ear exam to make sure the infection clears."

"Don't take this the wrong way," Rob said, "but I'm going to keep Dr. Taylor as Meredith's pediatrician. You always said she was one of the best."

"She is, and you should. Rob, I don't give a damn about being your baby's doctor," Doc said, his voice full of frustration. He gripped his son's shoulders and stood toe to toe, blue eyes to blue eyes. "But I sure as hell want to be her grandfather."

Chapter Seven

Neither Rob nor Tip spoke during the ride home. Meredith fell asleep just as they reached the house, and Rob carried her in to bed.

He was dead tired. He got a drink of water and went into the living room, where Tip sat on the sofa, chewing on her lower lip.

He dropped down next to her. After a while he said, "You're awfully quiet. What are you thinking about?"

She looked at him, incredulous. "Are you kidding? What do you think I'm thinking about?"

He closed his eyes and ran his fingers through his hair. "Geez, Tip, you're not going to want to talk about this thing with Doc, are you?"

"You have to admit, Rob, that this is a very strange situation. When was the last time you and your father were together, anyway? Birthday phone calls don't count."

"I don't know. My mother's funeral, I guess."

Tip let out a long breath. "Three years ago? What happened?"

"Nothing, really. I had moved out of the house years before, so I didn't see him that much as it was. I guess neither of us made the effort to keep the relationship going."

"Why ever not?" It was all but incomprehensible to Tip, whose family meant so much to her.

He shrugged. "He's busy, I'm busy—"

"And you're both stubborn."

"Something like that."

Remembering he had said he and his father were miles apart, Tip shook her head. "That's such a *guy* thing to do," she said, and her voice held not judgment, but regret. "I guess you do as good a job keeping in touch with your brothers. How many are there, anyway?"

"Four."

"Any wives? Children?"

"Nope. They're all pretty busy with their careers."

"What are they?"

"The oldest is an independent film producer in Los Angeles. Another is a Wall Street wonder, the third is an attorney in Boston, and the last is a journalist in Washington, D.C."

Tip raised one eyebrow. "A bunch of overachievers, and no one became a doctor like your father?"

"He wanted me to become his partner in his practice."

"Why you? Why not one of your brothers?" Tip's curiosity was piqued now.

"Because I was the one who was always hanging around his office."

Which told her that he felt closer to his father than he wanted to admit. "When did you decide to become a mechanic?"

"I always liked cars. When I was in high school, I decided to go to the tech school half days for auto mechanics. I liked hands-on work, which was part of the reason I was attracted to medicine. But I didn't want to give up my life for my profession."

Like his father had. He didn't say the words, but Tip could read between the lines.

He gave her a devilish grin. "Besides, I kind of liked being the failure of the family."

Not bothering to rise to the bait, Tip felt her respect for him jump another big notch. She knew what it was like to be looked at superficially. If his intellect was hidden by his choice of profession, she had a body that made people think she had the IQ of a ball of fluff.

Rob watched Tip as she frowned in thought again. She looked adorable, sitting there in her rumpled sweatsuit. It was uncanny. The closer he got to her, the more intrigued he became. It had always worked the opposite way with other women. The better he got to know them, the less he wanted to.

Apparently she had come to some kind of conclusion. "All right," she said decisively. "I can buy that you've drifted out of touch with your father and your brothers."

He gave a wry half smile.

But Tip wasn't finished. "But as Meredith's caretaker, I can't agree with your *staying* out of touch. She's already down to half a family, without a mother. She should have a chance to know her grandfather and her uncles. Do your brothers even know about her?"

"At least one of them does."

"Let me guess. The Boston attorney?"

Rob nodded. "I needed legal help. I imagine the rest have heard through him or Doc or someone else from town."

"You mean you didn't send out birth announcements?"

"*Birth* announcements!"

Tip looked at him through narrowed eyes. "Rob Winfield, are you ashamed of your daughter?"

That hit home, just like it was meant to. "Of course not," Rob said, annoyed. "I just hate to write."

"It's not too late," Tip said matter-of-factly. "Meredith should have one for her baby memory book, too."

Before Rob could speak, she added, "The one I'm going to get for you to keep a record of all the milestones in her life. After I sleep for a few hours, that is."

She stood up and stretched. The sun was up now, its rays slanting in the bay window and pooling at Tip's feet. "And while you're sending mail to your brothers, why don't you include an invitation to a family reunion?" If she was going to stick her nose in his business, she might as well do a thorough job of it. For Meredith's sake.

"A *what?*" Rob jumped to his feet.

Tip looked innocent. "It's about time, don't you think? Besides, they're all going to want to meet their niece," she said reasonably. "What do you think?"

"I think you're a pain in the neck."

She grinned. "And I think you're going to miss me when I'm gone."

"That's what you think," he called after her as she went off to bed. He wasn't going to miss her, because pain in the neck though she was, he wasn't about to let her get away.

After running some errands, Tip walked into the house and put a brand-new baby memory book on the table in front of Rob and Meredith. "See? There's lots of room for writing all about her."

Rob paged through the book, keeping it out of the reach of Meredith, who was eyeing up its potential for chewing. "You mean like first word and first step and stuff like that?"

"Yes, but not just the big things. You'll want to re-member the little things, too, like how she reaches for her crib mobile and splashes in the bathtub. And her favorite things, too—favorite toy, favorite food—"

"Favorite babysitter?" Rob put in dryly.

Tip grinned. "Sure. I'll even personally autograph it." Then the phone rang. "I'll get it," she said. "This will be Mary Kate calling to find out about last night." Last night? The meeting seemed like days ago, not hours.

"Did you meet anyone?" Mary Kate asked with-out preamble.

"Aren't you going to ask me if I found out about any job openings?" Tip asked.

"Did you?"

"No."

"That's too bad, Tip." Mary Kate sounded genu-inely sorry. After a few moments she perked up again. "But did you meet anyone?"

"I met a lot of people."

"Any men?"

"Yes."

"Any nice ones?"

"Yes."

Mary Kate's voice rose in excitement. "A good prospect? Was he interested in you?"

"He gave me his card."

"All right!" Mary Kate said enthusiastically. "When are you going to call him?"

"I'm not."

A few moments of silence was broken by Mary Kate's shriek. "Tip!"

Tip held the phone away from her ear. "Yes?"

"You drive me *crazy!*"

Tip smiled. "The feeling is mutual, little sister." She glanced at Rob and saw that he had stopped paging through the baby book and was looking at her, a broad grin on his face. She quickly put the phone next to her ear again.

Mary Kate had decided to let the matter drop. "Don't forget our family reunion is two weeks from today. Is that still all right for you?"

"Absolutely."

"Will your car be ready by then?"

Tip twirled the phone cord around her finger. "I'm not sure."

"Well, if you need a ride, Sean or Tommy will come and pick you up."

"I'll let you know."

When Tip hung up the phone, she found that Rob was still grinning at her. "What?" she said.

"I think your sister and I have a lot in common."

Tip laughed out loud. "You and Mary Kate?"

He beckoned her closer to where he sat. She bent down, and he cupped a hand around the back of her neck, guiding her ear to his lips. A shiver stole through her at the feel of his warm breath. Again. And yet again.

It was madness, this feeling. She should pull away. But something besides his gentle hand kept her right where she was.

At last, Rob spoke. "You drive me crazy, too," he whispered in her ear, then let her go.

In the warm August days that followed, Tip was happier than she had been in a long time. Rob and Meredith needed her, and it was a wonderful feeling, to be needed.

She liked Madison, too. Morning strolls with Meredith were anything but solitary. Strangers who came up to fuss over the baby soon became acquaintances. Nearly everyone knew Rob. She and the baby became "regulars" at the variety, and Tip liked that too, once she had made it politely clear that she wasn't interested in listening to or passing on gossip. Ned seemed to welcome their interruption of his video game, and after a while was able to keep playing without getting flustered. Now, he only got flustered when a certain someone behind the bakery counter looked his way. And no wonder. He had been dating Susie ever since the rhubarb pie.

Mysteriously, Tip and Meredith seemed to meet Doc every morning, as he finished up his jog. Tip loved to watch him lift Meredith from her stroller for a hug, closing his eyes to savor the moment. And Meredith didn't treat him like a stranger. She grabbed his nose and chewed on his chin just like she did to Tip and Rob.

Tip took Meredith over to the garage one afternoon, something else that had become almost a ritual for them.

Fred greeted her as usual. "Sure you haven't changed your mind about going out with me, doll? It's an experience you won't want to live without."

"I'll manage." Fred was annoying, but he was all talk, and as oddly endearing as Ned, though in a completely different way.

"I don't know," he said to Meredith, shaking his head. "Old Uncle Fred here is losing his touch with the ladies. Your lovely babysitter started it, and now that cute little blond at the variety just turned me down too. Only she says someone else got there first."

Tip looked at Ned, who smiled and shrugged. Apparently Fred didn't know his brother was the one who had gotten there first. She'd like to be there when he found out.

"Tell me someone got there first with you, too, doll," Fred said to Tip. "That will soothe my wounded ego."

Tip looked up to see Rob at the sink in the back, washing up, his broad shoulders straining the fabric of his T-shirt. She ignored Fred's question. "You'll find someone who will give your ego all the soothing it needs," she assured him.

Rob walked toward her, wiping his hands on a towel, and picked up his daughter. "What did you ladies do today?" he asked.

"Today was play group. And then we went to the library for some new board books." Tip looked around. "Is it my imagination or are you guys busier than ever lately?"

"I meant to talk with you about that. We've gotten in a slew of new customers, and most of them say they were referred by you."

"Meredith and I meet a lot of people," she said. "Just doing our part for the common good."

Rob was swooping Meredith through the air, which elicited delighted baby giggles from her. "You haven't asked about your car for a while," he said to Tip.

Tip blushed guiltily. She had been caught up in her day-to-day life with Meredith. Reveling in it. When her car was ready, it would all end, so no wonder she hadn't thought much about her car lately. "That's because I assume that you're going as fast as you can on it," she told him lightly.

"With all the business you've been referring to me, I'm having a hard time getting to your car," he said. The truth was, Rob had been dragging his feet on the repairs to her car. Not only because the garage had gotten so busy, but because, quite frankly, he wanted to keep Tip there as long as he could. And not just for Meredith's sake.

"Well, I won't really need it until the end of the month, when the fall sessions at most places start," Tip said. "And besides fixing my car, you need time to find a good situation for Meredith, when I'm gone."

"Yes," Rob said, but the single word left a sour taste in his mouth. There was no better situation for Meredith than the one they had right now, and he knew it.

The next day when Rob came home from work, he heard laughter coming from the kitchen. He found Tip sitting at the table, which was covered with books and papers. With her was Jessie, one of the girls from her babysitting class.

Rob greeted them and shimmied past Tip's chair to the playpen and Meredith, who wiggled with delight when she saw him. Picking her up and maneuvering his way back around the table gave him an excuse to brush against Tip. He had to admit that a small house did have its advantages, contact-wise.

"What's doing, ladies? Don't tell me you needed a refresher course already," he teased.

"Oh, we're not doing baby stuff, Mr. Winfield," Jessie answered. "Tip is tutoring me in math."

"I see." Rob spoke to Jessie, but looked at Tip.

Jessie wrinkled her nose. "If I flunk math in summer school, I'll have to take it again this year with kids who are a grade behind me."

"That's incentive. Go to it," he said. And with a secret wink at Tip, he left them alone.

When he heard Jessie leave, he brought Meredith back into the kitchen and settled her in the playpen. "So tell me," he said, sitting next to Tip. He took her hand in his and started massaging her palm with the pad of his thumb. "How's the job search going?"

Tip felt her hand, and the rest of her, relax with the gentle pressure of his caress. "Lots of outgoing résumés, no incoming responses," she said.

"Mind if I make a suggestion?"

"As long as you don't mind if I ignore it."

Rob smiled to himself. "Have you ever thought about teaching kids who are younger than college age?"

"You mean high school?"

"I was thinking a bit younger."

"Middle school?" She leveled a gaze at him. "Do you have any idea what people say about teaching in middle school?"

"No, but I imagine most adults find it a particularly tough age group to relate to. And I have seen for myself that you are not one of them."

Tip was silent, but she continued to respond to his touch. A cloud of warmth spread within her. "I never really thought about it," she said slowly.

"You'd be good. You'd probably even have fun."

Tip sounded interested. "Well, I can't say I ever loved academia. I love math, though, and I love teaching it. And middle school is a particularly crucial time to keep kids interested in it. Especially girls."

"You'd be a great role model," Rob said coaxingly.

Suddenly Tip stiffened under his hands. "I can't do it anyway," she said abruptly, pulling her hand away and rising to her feet. She, Tip Padderson, a role model for sticking with something? "I don't have the certification," she told him.

Rob stepped back, holding up both hands. "Hey, it was just an idea."

"Thank you, but I'm afraid it's an idea I can't use," she said, leaving the room, and leaving Rob to wonder whether he would ever understand this woman.

A tiny sound in the night woke Tip up instantly. She opened her eyes, waiting while they adjusted to the darkness in her room. Again she heard a soft baby whimper. And again. As her father, Rob had an unspoken claim on going to Meredith in the night. But when she heard Meredith fuss a fourth time, Tip decided he must be too tired to wake up. She padded barefoot into the baby's room and lifted her gently from the crib.

Meredith was half-asleep herself, her face scrunched into a tiny look of displeasure. She was wet from head to toe.

There was enough moonlight streaming in the open window that Tip didn't need to turn a light on to change the baby and strip the wet sheet off the crib. She threw a new one in and put Meredith on it in the center of the crib while she tucked the four corners under the mattress. Then she leaned on the side of the crib, watching Meredith rub her eyes, proud of the job she had done.

She was good at this, and she knew it. She loved doing for Meredith everything that a mother would, even the dirty work. Being with the baby paid all of that back, tenfold and more. Nothing, absolutely nothing Tip had done in her life could hold a candle to this.

And this would all be over soon. Rob would finish her car, and she would have to leave, and she would never again have the chance to do this. She wouldn't be able to share Meredith's life, to watch her grow up. She would most likely never have a baby of her own to fuss over and worry over and smile over with a loving husband. A man like Rob.

A man like that deserved the best in a wife; and as a wife, Tip had been a disaster.

Tears started to fill her eyes, but she brushed them away impatiently. Why was she wasting a golden opportunity? This may well be her only chance to perform one of life's most precious acts of kindness, and share a bond with loving parents through the generations: to soothe an infant who needed human warmth and bonding in the middle of the night, to rock her gently back to sleep. She picked up Meredith, who was still rubbing her eyes and whimpering, and carried her over to the rocking chair.

Secure against Tip's shoulder, Meredith snuggled right in and began to settle down. Tip hummed softly as she rocked, her eyes closed, the better to savor the warm sensations running through her.

Some time later—maybe minutes, maybe hours— she felt Rob's hand on her shoulder. She opened her eyes to find him standing beside the rocking chair, his bare upper body gleaming like marble in the moonlight. He dropped to his knees next to the chair, his arm resting comfortably on her shoulders, looking at the baby.

Tip wondered at the way he touched her. He seemed to do it all the time lately, ever since that night in his father's house, when he had put his arm around her. Since then he had touched her countless times and in countless ways. But never in a way that made her feel threatened.

It was a first. Because of the way she was put together, men had tried to touch her all the time, and she had always hated it. Even with Michael. Like the others, he didn't do it for her, but for himself.

Rob, on the other hand, was unselfish with his touches. He seemed to want to make her feel good. And he did.

Not that she thought he was oblivious to the way she was built, despite the fact that she had become an expert at hiding it. He knew. He had known from the first. And she had known, after seeing that calendar in his office, that he was certainly the kind of man who appreciated a body like hers.

But in all fairness, she had to admit that he was also the kind of man who appreciated a witty remark. And how well she took care of his daughter, and how good she had been with the girls from babysitting class. Maybe Rob Winfield didn't fit the mold after all.

So she sat in the darkness, with his sleeping daughter in her arms, and savored the feel of his gentle touch. She didn't know where he was going with this. But she knew one thing. For the first time ever, she was inclined to stick around and find out.

After he left them, silently, Tip tucked Meredith into her crib and kissed her on the forehead. She didn't feel like going to bed; she wanted to be part of the moonlit night, so she stepped out onto the deck.

"Hello," a low voice greeted her.

As her eyes adjusted, she saw Rob standing at the other end of the deck. She walked over to him. "I thought you had gone back to bed."

"I'm not as tired now as I was before. I can't believe I didn't hear Meredith. Thanks for going in to her."

Tip dismissed his thanks with a wave of her hand.

He knew why he had slept through Meredith's cry. Having Tip there in the house was comforting. He could trust her with his precious baby.

But so many pieces of the puzzle that was Tip didn't seem to fit. "Tip," he said finally. "What is it you are looking for?"

She purposely misunderstood his question. "I'm looking for a job. You know that," she said with a little laugh.

"Is that all you want? What about marriage, a home, a family of your own?"

"That's a loaded question."

Rob wondered what in the world she meant. "It's a *simple* question," he pointed out.

"Maybe. But there are no simple answers," she murmured.

"You'd be a great mother," he observed.

She shook her head, and a small sound escaped her, one of pain or frustration; he didn't know which.

"You're such a natural at taking care of Meredith."

She sighed, a sad smile playing around her lips. "Meredith is incredible."

"But you don't want to be a mother."

She swallowed. "I never said that," she told him. Wanting had nothing to do with it. Babies needed mommies who could stay in one place. And their daddies needed wives who could keep them satisfied. "My life has simply... gone down another path."

"So change paths."

"Trust me, it's not that easy." You couldn't change who you were. Despite all of her running from it, her past only seemed to loom larger up ahead of her. Tip started to leave.

Rob's voice came softly. "No, I suppose not. Not nearly as easy as running away." Then he added the single word that had stopped her at Doc's. "Stay."

Maybe it was the raw edge of need in his voice. Or the contradictory softness of his request. Whatever it was, it made the impulse to take off, which normally reigned supreme in Tip, melt away as if by magic. She stayed.

Side by side, they looked off into the woods for some time. "People can really make a mess of their lives," she said finally. "And the past does have a way of coming back to haunt you." She should know. Lately hers had been haunting her like never before.

"Only if you let it," Rob said. "Past mistakes are what you make of them. Sometimes they're not mistakes at all."

"What do you mean?"

"Good things can come of them."

"Ah," she said, understanding. "Good things like Meredith?"

He nodded. "She's the best thing that ever happened to me. That's what I mean. My daughter is not a 'mistake,' but it wasn't exactly a planned pregnancy. If you had asked my opinion then, I would have said that the *last* thing I wanted was to be a father. I took every precaution not to be. Even though Sondra had told me she was on the pill, I used protection. Every time."

Tip felt herself start to shake. Her stomach churned.

Rob looked at her. "Are you all right?" When she didn't answer, he went on. "I guess that's why she didn't bother telling me she had gone off the pill to lose weight when she wanted to be a model. Still, one time, what I was using failed."

Tip pulled away and started to walk into the house. Rob moved quickly into her path. What the hell was the matter with her? He thought women were supposed to like it when men opened up and got all sensitive and everything. "Where are you going?" he asked in a harsh voice.

"I . . . I've got to go in," she said, shakily.

Didn't she realize how much this was costing him? Not that he needed anyone's sympathy; he simply wanted her to know the truth. He crossed his arms over his chest. "Hey, do you think I talk about this with just anyone? As someone who once questioned my control over my sexual urges, the least you can do is stand here and listen," he said, not bothering to hide his anger.

Tip knew he was right, but she couldn't find it in her to be the sympathetic listener right now. She was caught up in the sudden turmoil of her own emotions.

When she didn't say anything, Rob shook his head. "Talk about mistakes," he said, in a voice edged with sarcasm. "Real smart of me, not to have just let you walk away the first time."

Tip's rational side knew he had a right to be upset, but it lost the struggle with her emotional side. If he was feeling hurt, he wasn't the only one. Angry and aching inside, she blurted out, "Can't you see? I just don't want to think about you making love to another woman!"

Both were shocked at what she had said. They went still and silent, standing there inches apart looking at each other, their breathing labored.

Tip was terrified at the unknown depth of her feelings.

Rob's surprise turned to wonder. Did she mean another woman, as in, a woman other than *herself?* He felt the blood humming through his body, but at the same time realized that this was not the time to call her on it. She was white as a ghost, and poised for flight.

"It was tactless of me to bring up the subject," he offered. "Like I said, I've never shared that with anyone." He hoped that that meant something to her.

Tip had gotten herself under control again. "How silly of me to react that way," she said in a carefully matter-of-fact tone. She even managed a short, dry laugh at her own expense. "Of course I knew that you and Sondra had—" She swallowed. "Had made love, in order for Meredith to be here."

At that moment, Rob was drawn to her as never before. He wanted—no, *needed*—to touch her, but he knew that might drive her away. He was struck with the sudden realization that he had never made love—not with Sondra, not with any woman—in his life. But standing there in the darkness with Tip, he began to realize what had been missing before.

He had never thought of himself as the kind for moonlight confessions. But he was an honest man, and some things just had to be said. "You know what my biggest mistake was?" he said softly.

She shook her head.

"Making love to a woman I didn't love."

He felt Tip gather herself and step away, and knew he wasn't going to be able to stop her from leaving. This time. So he stood and watched her disappear into his house.

Late on Friday afternoon, Rob was in the office, talking on the phone with a supplier. Suddenly he heard Tip calling for him from the house through the open window.

"Rob! Get off the phone and get over here. Quick!"

He hung up and sprinted across the side yard to the house, his heart pounding. Tip was standing on the deck, waiting impatiently. Meredith was nowhere to be seen.

"What's wrong? Where is she?"

Tip led him into the house. "She's gone mobile!" she said excitedly as they went down the hall.

"You've gone nuts. What are you talking about?"

Tip pointed to the crib triumphantly. Meredith, lying there on her back, looked at her grown-ups and gave them a big beamer.

"See?" Tip said. She was beaming, too.

Rob just stared at her.

"Don't you get it? After I changed her, I put her in here on her stomach while I put a few things away. When I looked at her again, she was like this."

"She rolled over? By herself?" Rob's voice was full of wonder. He went over and placed the baby gently on her stomach. Meredith turned her head up to look at him, and with a push of her arm and a twist of her leg she rolled over onto her back again.

Grinning, Rob bent down and kissed her. "Wow," he said.

"I thought she could do it again," Tip said proudly.

Rob straightened up. "You mean you didn't try it before you called for me?"

Tip looked at him with scorn. "Of course not. You're her father. You should be the one to experience these milestones with her."

At that moment, Rob knew that he loved this woman, just as surely and irrevocably as he loved his baby. He reached Tip in one giant step, swooping her up in his arms and spinning around the room with her, savoring the sound of her laughter. From her crib, Meredith just stared at them.

He came to a dead stop in the middle of the room. Tip's eyes locked with his as he slowly slid her down the front of him and placed her back on her feet. They looked at each other for four thudding heartbeats, then he folded her into his arms for a full frontal hug. They stood there, body to body, embracing to the tune of the baby they both loved cooing softly in her crib.

Rob felt Tip melt into the hug. He kissed her on the top of the head, and drew immense satisfaction from the fact that he was the first one to pull away. That didn't mean he wanted to. He did it for her.

He looked down at her. Even with his own eyes filled with love, it was easy to read her face as she stood looking at him, her eyes large and wondrous.

Talk about a milestone.

Chapter Eight

It wasn't long before Tip decided to ask Rob to do something with her that she had never done with any man.

She invited him to her family reunion.

On Sunday they packed up the Jeep, strapped Meredith into her car seat and set out for Hartford.

"I'm glad you asked us to come with you," Rob said.

"I'm glad you wanted to."

After a pause, he said, "Before we get much further, shouldn't you be filling me in on any deep, dark secrets?"

Tip felt her heart drop into her shoes. She wasn't ready for this. "What do you mean?" she asked, apprehensively.

He glanced at her and grinned. "You know. Skeletons in the closet, subjects you're not supposed to bring up. Most families have them. You're not holding back on me, are you?''

Tip gave a relieved laugh, and answered truthfully, ''Why would I hold anything back about my family? They're terrific.''

''Tell me more about them.''

''Sean is married to a wonderful woman named Terri. He's a CPA.''

''Another numbers person.''

''It runs in the family. We got the math gene from my mother, who did bookkeeping for a company down the road from home. I still don't know how she managed, as a young widow with three little kids.'' Tip smiled. ''But nothing was too much for Mom. She would have loved being a grandmother.''

''Do Sean and Terri have any kids?''

''Alanna, who's two.''

''Pretty name.''

''She was named after my father, Alan Padderson.''

Rob turned onto the highway. ''Do you miss him?''

''I was only four when he died, too young to remember much about him. But Mom always told us about him. I sure missed getting a chance to know him. I missed having a father.'' And she didn't only miss having a father when she was a child. She missed having a father now, as an adult, and thought of Doc with envy.

''And then there's Mary Kate. I feel like I know her already,'' Rob said with a smile.

''My little sister.''

''She got the math gene too?''

''Yes. She went into computers, and found a job she loves and a terrific husband. She and Tommy have twin one-year-olds, Pammie and Will. Meredith is going to love them.''

Meredith did love them, and Alanna too. She watched the older children, fascinated, as they walked, crawled, ran and played. Not to mention swam and splashed, because Mary Kate and Tommy had a pool in their backyard.

Rob took Meredith in with him, holding her in his arms as he did when they went in the pool at home. Other than that, he didn't see much of her. Tip was busy showing her off to her family, all of whom wanted a turn holding her, too.

He smiled to himself when he noticed that Tip kept an eye on him as he talked with different people. He was no fool. He didn't need the reaction of her brother, her sister or their spouses to tell him that Tip had granted him a real privilege by inviting him to meet the family that obviously meant so much to her.

The best part was, he didn't have to pretend to have a good time. The women teased him about fatherhood as if they'd known him all his life, and when he went out front with Tommy and Sean to look at their cars, he keenly felt the time he had missed with his own brothers. While they were out there, they gave him a subtle brotherly warning about taking care of Tip. Far from being insulted, he had expected it, and would have been disappointed if they hadn't issued it.

Miraculously, after the food was put away, all the kids went down for a nap at the same time. Meredith was sleeping in her portable crib in the twins' room. Rob found himself sitting next to Mary Kate at one end of the pool, with the baby monitor positioned between their deck chairs. Tip sat at the other end of the pool, dangling her feet in the water. Everyone else was swimming.

"This is the first chance I've had to talk with you," Mary Kate commented.

"Thanks for having me," Rob said.

"Are you kidding? I was thrilled when Tip wanted to bring you."

"I think she's enjoyed showing off Meredith."

Mary Kate laughed. "Understatement of the year. I haven't seen her so happy in…" She paused. "Well, you can probably imagine how long."

Rob was glad to hear that Tip was happy living with him and Meredith, but disturbed by her sister's implication that she hadn't been before. It hinted at the sadness he had seen in her eyes since he'd known her. It hinted at the reasons for her running.

Since Tip was obviously cheerful by nature, he wondered what was eating at her. But he would find out from her, not by asking Mary Kate.

Instead, he changed the subject. He looked at the pool. "You certainly are a family of swimmers."

Mary Kate laughed. "It was hard not to be, since Mom was the coach of our swim team."

Rob felt a niggling suspicion but didn't say anything.

"Of course, Tip was always the best," Mary Kate went on. "She outswam every other girl in town, and most of the boys, too. She claims she swam so much she got waterlogged, but I still can't imagine why she hasn't gone in at all the past few years."

Rob looked at Tip sitting at the other end of the pool, safely covered up as usual, in an oversized T-shirt over her long shorts. He wasn't exactly sure either, but he could make a wild guess.

At that, the babies woke up, and reclaimed their rightful place as the center of attention. Later in the afternoon, the food appeared again. It was getting dark when Tip and Rob got themselves and a yawning Meredith into the car to go home. The last person to hug Tip goodbye was Mary Kate. Then she leaned in the car window and whispered, "Now I know why you threw that other guy's business card away."

If Rob heard, he gave no indication of it as they drove away. Mary Kate was right, of course, but she wasn't telling Tip anything she didn't already know. Rob had only had to look at her from across the pool today to start her insides humming. Sitting here next to him, the force of the attraction seemed to make the air between them crackle. He rested his hand on her thigh. After a few minutes, she covered it with hers.

"Are you glad you came?" she asked, looking at his profile in the glow of the dashboard light.

"I wouldn't have missed it."

"Isn't my family terrific?" Tip asked, excited. "Can you see why I call them so much?"

He smiled and gave her thigh a squeeze. "I may be tempted to call them myself, now that I know them," he teased. "I did call my own, though."

Tip sat up straight. "Your own what?"

"Family. I called all my brothers and told them about Meredith."

She reached over and hugged him so hard he had to put his other hand back on the steering wheel to keep from veering off the road. "That's wonderful, Rob!"

"And they can come to the reunion."

"You're having a reunion?"

"They all agreed it was a great idea. Your idea."

Tip laughed out loud. "Rob, I'm so happy for you! And Meredith. And Doc," she said excitedly. "When will it be?"

"The only date we could agree on was Labor Day."

"Ah." Tip tried not to show her disappointment as she settled back into her seat. She wanted to meet his family, wanted *him* to want her to meet his family. But, of course, she would be gone before then.

Rob glanced over at her. "Consider this your official invitation, Tip. I'd really like you to be there."

Tip swallowed down the lump that had formed in her throat, the lump that was making it difficult to breathe, let alone talk. "If I can, I will," she said finally.

A few nights later, she had the dream again.

It was terrifying in its clarity, and in its predictability. The bright lights shining hot on her naked skin, exposing her to, and blinding her to, the men watching her from the surrounding darkness. Their voices, murmuring, jeering, shouting. Her feet, rooted to the ground. Her screams, piercing in the brightness, swallowed by the darkness. The desperate need for help.

But this night, the pattern changed. She wasn't awakened by her own screams, to find herself shaking in terror. Instead, her screams subsided along with the clamor from the dream men; and the brightness gradually dimmed, and the darkness lightened; and sight and sound merged into a oneness where she found peace, and sleep.

When Tip woke up later in the night and found that she wasn't alone in bed, she didn't startle or pull away.

There was no need to. She knew this touch; it was Rob. He was lying behind her, curled on his side like she was, cradling her with his body, enfolding her in his arms.

Rob was the reason the dream had ended differently this time. He must have heard her screams, and come to her while she slept. He had taken her away from the nightmare.

She listened to his deep, even breathing. She smelled his familiar, masculine scent. She felt his warmth against her back, the weight of his arm around her.

She lay there, thinking that the old Tip would have been halfway to anywhere by now. But she couldn't even consider leaving. Where could she go? There was nowhere on earth she would rather be.

She slept.

The next time she woke up it was morning. Early sunlight was slanting through the blinds, Meredith was cooing happily in her crib, and Rob was still lying next to her in her bed. But now he was awake. He was propped up on one elbow, looking at her with all the intensity of his blue eyes.

"Good morning," he said softly, and pulled her into his arms. Their folded knees straightened as they drew closer, their bodies melding so powerfully that they both began to tremble.

He eased away slightly, but not before the hardness of his body had impressed itself upon her. Now, with effort, there was space between them. But she kept her hand on his side, and felt his stroking up and down her back. When his breathing lost its ragged edge, he spoke again, his voice deep and compelling.

"If you could overlook the circumstances, there is something I would like to ask you," he began.

Tip quelled her sudden urge to laugh. They were lying together in bed, wearing a combined total of a T-shirt and a pair of shorts, fresh from an embrace that had just about made the aforementioned garments history. Circumstances like that were pretty hard to overlook.

"This is hardly a conventional way to ask a woman for a first date, but—" His slight hesitation was disarming. "I would like to take you out for dinner tonight."

Rob made all the arrangements for their first official date, from flowers to dinner reservations. And he arranged for a babysitter—Doc, who arrived early with a broad smile on his face.

Tip was wearing a matching grin, Rob noticed. For that matter, he was pretty pleased himself. Doc had been thrilled at the chance to spend some time with his granddaughter, who wiggled and kicked when she saw him, and went willingly from Rob's arms to his. Tip had been right about families. This felt good.

Doc was pleased about the Labor Day reunion, too. His first reaction had been a dry, "I wonder whose idea that was," smiling at Tip. But he was clearly looking forward to having his sons all together, and said he wouldn't miss the reunion for the world.

Rob was feeling on top of the world. His life, the one that had been blown to bits by Sondra's pregnancy, was coming back together, bit by bit, even better than before. And the best part of it was sitting in his Jeep right next to him, with the wind from her open window whipping her wild red hair all over the place.

Tip had agreed to go out on a date with him, and as far as he was concerned, that changed the rules. Before, he had had plenty of qualms about touching her like a lover. All gone, now.

He would have to take it slowly, of course. And he had a feeling he knew why. But that was another thing. The next rule to go was the no-asking-personal-questions rule. There were a lot of things he needed to know about Tip, things he had a feeling no one else, not even Mary Kate, knew.

"You look pretty," he told her, while to himself he added, *but why do you hide your beautiful figure?*

"Thanks," she said shyly. She didn't return the compliment, but then, she didn't have to. He had seen her looking at him—when she trusted herself to look at him at all, that is—like she'd like to have him for dinner. Which led Rob to another question: *What are you so afraid of that you have to hold back like that?*

And then there was the biggie, the million-dollar-jackpot question. *How can I make you want to stay?*

Best to start with smaller things, though. Over dinner he said, "There's something I've been wanting to ask you all day."

Tip looked up at him, her eyes glowing. "About that letter that came for me? It's about a job opening."

Rob felt the pit of his stomach drop. That wasn't what he was going to ask. He summoned up the enthusiasm to ask, "Really? Where?"

He breathed again when Tip answered, "Just forty-five minutes away. At a junior college."

"Sounds like just what you were looking for."

"Actually, I've been looking into your idea about middle school. But getting my certification will take a while, and right now I need something that will pay the bills. As of yet, I don't know if this one will. I'll find out details at my interview tomorrow afternoon. That is, if it's all right with you," she said, frowning.

"Tip, I'm glad you felt free to set up an interview. Friday afternoon is perfect. I can be with Meredith."

Rob couldn't believe his luck. Tip could be looking at jobs anywhere in the country. For her to find one within commuting distance was another stroke of the luck that seemed to be running his way lately.

It was a muggy, moonless night, still warm when they got home and sent Doc on his way. Since he had opened the pool, Rob had tried unsuccessfully to get Tip to come out with him at night while he swam. Tonight, after checking on Meredith and scooping up the monitor, he simply took Tip's hand and led her out to the pool.

They sat side by side, dangling their feet in the water next to the ladder. Then Rob lifted Tip up and settled her sideways across his lap. For an instant, she saw in his eyes what she then felt on his lips as he pressed them to hers.

They had progressed far beyond the point of their first kiss. This one was deep and lush and overflowing with unexpressed feelings, feelings that had been building over all those weeks of living together. Tip felt an urgency in Rob that matched her own, but at the same time, his kiss was unhurried, undemanding.

For Tip, whose past experience in such things had largely been forced on her, the softness of Rob's lips was a revelation. The velvety stroking of his tongue, a wonder. And the touch of his hands redefined masculinity not in terms of strength used, but strength possessed.

When the kiss finally broke off, eyes took over where lips had left off. And it seemed to Tip that Rob's looked straight into her soul. They remained poised like that; and she waited, savoring her own eagerness, her deep need, for another kiss.

"Have you caught your breath, sweetheart?" he breathed into her ear. She nodded, and he shifted her in his arms until he was holding her out over the pool, his muscles tense with the effort. Then he slowly lowered her to the surface of the water and gently released her.

When the water closed over her, Tip stopped savoring and started sinking. Then she swam, surfaced, and blew a mouthful of water at Rob, who was still sitting at the side of the pool.

"What was that for?" she asked, fully realizing how hard it was to look threatening while you are treading water, and your shirt is billowing up all around you on top of the water.

"For making an honest woman of you."

A few smooth strokes took her to the side of the pool. She grabbed on to the wall next to him. "I never told you I didn't know how to swim. I told you that I *didn't* swim."

"I know."

"I imagine someone in my family told you that I used to swim," she went on.

"No one in your family knows why you stopped."

She did her best to look annoyed, though her heart was pounding. "And you do?"

"I'm betting it's the same reason why you didn't climb out of the pool right now, with me here watching, knowing that your wet clothes will be plastered right against your body. The body you try desperately to hide with the baggy clothes you wear.''

Tip was speechless, shocked by how well he had seen through this part of her.

He eased into the water next to her, clothes and all, his eyes issuing a challenge. ''Tell me I'm wrong,'' he said softly.

Tip looked away.

Gently, Rob led her into shallower water, where they could both stand. He pulled her into his arms, swearing softly above her head into the warm night air. ''We men can be such bastards,'' he said.

Tip didn't say anything, but she wrapped her arms tightly around him.

''Tip, you have a beautiful body. You have a slim waist, a firm, rounded bottom, and large, exquisitely shaped breasts. There is nothing wrong with that.''

''There is something wrong when your looks have an impact on the way people see you,'' she said.

''We men are usually out to get whatever we can,'' he said, kissing her on the top of her head.

''I can't help the way I'm built.'' Some tears escaped, lost on her wet face. ''Men could never see beyond that.'' Not even the man who had taken marriage vows with her.

''We men can be blind idiots sometimes.''

Tip pulled back and looked up at him. ''You don't have to take the collective guilt of manhood upon yourself.''

''No?''

''You're different, Rob,'' she argued. ''I think you can see beyond the outside. I think you like *me*.''

''Go on.''

She stopped, puzzled.

"Don't you see? That's the whole point," he said gently. He pulled back and looked into her eyes. "You're not just a body to me, Tip. You're the woman who has brought meaning to my life. You're the woman whose fine mind stimulates me. You're the woman I love to talk with and laugh with and be with. You're the woman who gives loving care to my daughter. You're the woman I want to make happy."

Tip swallowed. "I am?"

"You are. Of course, all that doesn't mean I'm not interested in your body, too," he warned. "But I'll take it as slow as you like."

Tip's heart started pounding again, but not from terror this time. This morning was not a good indication of her inclination to take things slowly. It had been easy to deny her sensuality before. But with Rob, it would not be denied. And here she was, next to him, with water gently lapping around them. Reason was about to take wing.

Rob led her to the shallow end and sat her down next to him on the steps, with his arm around her. "When I told you I was wondering about something today, it wasn't about the letter you'd gotten."

"No? What did you want to know?"

"What you were dreaming about last night, when you started screaming."

Tip felt herself tense up. "It's this nightmare I have. I . . , I'm not dressed."

"Ah, Tip, sweetheart," he crooned.

"And there are men watching. Lots of them. And I'm under bright lights. And I want to run, but I can't get away."

He held her close. "You relaxed when I came in and held you and talked to you. I'll do that every time it happens, until—"

"Until what?"

"Until you don't have that dream anymore," he finished simply.

Would she ever not have that dream anymore? Over the past five years it had woven itself into the very fabric of her existence, firmly binding past to present.

"Do you know what I wanted to do, when I was in bed with you this morning?" Rob asked.

Tip came back to the present with a blush, remembering what she had felt as they had embraced. "I hate to have to break this to you, but it wouldn't have taken a genius to figure that out," she said dryly.

He chuckled low, against her ear. "I mean besides that," he said.

"No. What?"

"I wanted to bring Meredith in bed with us."

Tip knew that he brought the baby into his own bed in the early morning. Often when she got up to use the bathroom, she heard Meredith cooing from Rob's room. At times, she had stood outside the door and pictured the two of them snuggling and playing in the covers on his big bed, wishing she had the right to open the door and join them.

"I would really like that. Would you?" he asked, his voice itself a caress.

"Yes," Tip breathed, and all at once she realized that not only did Rob and Meredith need her; she needed them. She had been so stubbornly independent for so long, it was a new and wonderful feeling, to let herself need someone.

She turned to look at him, and slowly brought her hands up to the sides of his face. It was true. She needed this man, this man who had saved her from the dream, who needed her. He had made her need him. And more.

He had made her love him. Yes, *love* him. She had feared it, she had fought it, but there was no denying that she felt a deep and abiding love for the man.

He said it first.

"I love you," he said tenderly, his voice reverberating with the layers of emotion wrapped around those simple words.

She moved her mouth slowly toward his, shaking with the need to initiate a physical bond instead of running from one.

"And I love you," she breathed, right before her lips settled on his.

It was her kiss, from the beginning, and he let her determine the angle, the pressure, the motion and the depth, until their tongues joined fully and the kiss ceased to be hers, and became theirs. Her heart sang with a richness that echoed through her whole body as she gave herself to him in a way she had never given herself before.

When the kiss ended, they were both trembling. While they caught their breath, he smoothed his palms up and down her back. She found that she loved the feel of his hands. He didn't seem to be able to keep them off her, or keep them still. He moved one to her breast, caressing her hardened nipple through the clingy wet fabric of her shirt.

"Do you know how beautiful you are?" he said.

He dropped his mouth to her breast, and she gasped at the warmth and pressure as he drew her inside his mouth. Her head tilted back, her breath caught in wonder.

He pulled his mouth away, his smile gentle. "You didn't know that what gives me pleasure does the same for you."

She caught his hand and put it to her other breast. "No. But I'm a fast learner."

He chuckled, then captured her mouth for another deep kiss, while at the same time his hand kneaded her. His mouth caught her moans of pleasure, as he devoured her lips and caressed her tongue.

She moved her hand gently along his thigh, her pleasure more complete as she noticed that her light touch made his breath catch.

A crackle of static came from the baby monitor, and they both stopped and lifted their heads, listening. Meredith whimpered softly, then settled down to sleep again.

"She's part of this," he said after a moment.

"I love her, too," Tip said. It was true. If Meredith were her own flesh and blood, she couldn't love her any more.

"I know you do. And you know what she means to me. This isn't easy to say, Tip. But you have to know, I won't let her be hurt."

She knew exactly what he was talking about, and her voice of self-doubt answered him. "I'm not known for my staying power."

Incredibly, he smiled. "Sweetheart, there's nothing wrong with your staying power."

She looked at him, incredulous. "But you know that I'm always leaving."

"Yes. And knowing you, you must have had a good reason for it."

Tip felt her burden, the one she had been laboring under for five years, start to lighten. Before, sharing it would have made it even heavier. But now, she wanted to share it, with him. "I did," she whispered.

"So the only question is whether you *want* to stay."

Tip knew it wasn't that simple. She needed to tell him all about her failed marriage, her inadequacies, the whole painful past that had started her on the run. "Rob, I—"

Just then, Meredith came over the monitor again. She was crying this time, loud and clear and in earnest. Rob grabbed Tip's hand and helped her out of the pool. Clothes dripping, they walked swiftly over the grass toward the house.

"You are wonderful for Meredith," he said. "You have so much to share with her—your intelligence, your strength, your warmth, your values."

Tip's voice was urgent. "Rob—"

He stopped suddenly, and turned to her. "You know," he said huskily, "it's just as well she interrupted what was about to happen between us."

Tip couldn't pretend she didn't know what he meant. She didn't need his sudden, hard kiss, or his hand cupped against her bottom, to make it clear. At his touch, her thoughts scattered. She craved his every touch, and her newly awakened body—for so long her enemy, now becoming her ally—was aching to explore his. She was ready for that intimacy. And he could hardly make a secret of the fact that he felt the same way.

What's more, he had said he loved her, which fulfilled his new requirement, that he wouldn't make love to a woman he didn't love.

"Why is that just as well?" she asked, mystified.

He gave her a smile so full of love and longing, it made her heart thump against her ribs.

"Because I've just made my standards a notch tougher," he said, and she felt her heart stop when he paused and lowered his voice. "Even though I love you, I'm not going to make love with a woman I'm not married to."

Chapter Nine

The next afternoon, when Tip walked into the cool darkness of the garage, she found it empty and eerily quiet. Then she remembered that Rob let Fred and Ned go home early on Fridays, which meant he was here alone.

She took a deep breath. It was time. Telling Rob that she loved him had been easy compared to this, but it was time he knew all about her marriage and divorce. Before they could think about the future, he had to know about her past.

Rob sat in his office, trying to do paperwork. But despite the pages in front of him, all he could see was Tip. How she had looked last night, with wet clothes clinging to her beautiful body that trembled with need for him. Her wide gray eyes, soft with innocence, then half-closed with desire. Her lips, against his own, in a kiss of completion.

He had known all along that she was the ideal mother for his daughter. Strong-willed and intelligent, yet gentle and loving, possessing both the essence of fun and the essence of goodness.

But there was more. He had fallen in love with her himself. He loved her mind, he loved her body. He even loved her insecurity about her body, which his love would help her get over, in time.

He looked up to find her standing in the doorway of the office, all dressed up from her job interview, watching him with a face radiant with love, yet clouded with uncertainty.

"Hi," she said. The word was no more than a whisper, but it penetrated to his innermost core.

Without a word he went around the desk and pulled her into his arms. Their bodies aligned for a perfect fit, and Rob breathed in the sweet, womanly fragrance of the wild red hair that he loved. "Welcome home."

"I went to the house and found Doc there with Meredith. He told me you were over here."

Rob smiled. "I asked Doc if he would babysit again. I have a strong feeling you and I might have something to celebrate tonight."

She didn't answer, but he felt her arms tighten around him.

"Doc offered to come over early to give me a chance to get a little work done." He chuckled. "I should have known it would be a lost cause. All I could do was look at dates."

Tip glanced at his calendar. There was a picture of a race car on it, not a naked woman. "What happened to your other calendar?"

"It offended my woman. I had it terminated."

She had to smile. "My hero."

"You should have seen me. I was ruthless." Rob didn't see the need to mention that he had seen Fred digging it out of the trash can to take home. "Now, don't keep me waiting. How was your interview?"

She pulled back so she could look up at him, but he kept her hands enfolded in his. "I liked the place," she confessed. "The position is for teaching night classes."

Rob squeezed her hands. Their luck was still running strong and true. "Teaching at night? Tip, that's perfect. If you got the job, you could still be with Meredith during the day."

"They already offered me the job."

Rob let out a whoop, and pulled her back for another hug. "Way to go, sweetheart. I'm so happy for you. And for me."

At that moment, Tip realized that she, too, was as happy for his sake as she was for herself. Maybe that was part of loving. Like understanding was.

Which reminded her. It was time. She cleared her throat. "Rob, we need to talk about something," she began.

"I'll say we do. I'm thrilled about your job, but I was planning on our celebrating something else tonight." He looked at her meaningfully. "I have something to ask you, and although this might not be the place, it is most definitely the time."

Tip felt her heart fluttering around in her chest like a trapped bird. "Rob, wait."

"Wait? What for? This is inevitable, sweetheart." He spoke matter-of-factly, so convinced, so convincing. Then he gave her that crooked grin that never failed to make her heart squeeze. "I didn't hear you saying 'wait' last night."

Tip held up her hand. Real life, her life, was more complicated than that. "It's not that simple," she started to protest.

He cut off her words with a kiss. "Yes, it is. Simple question. Simple, one-word answer."

And then, right there in his office, he got down on one knee.

"The question is mine," he said, taking her hands in his. "Tip, will you marry me?"

She looked at the man she loved kneeling in front of her, his clear blue eyes shining with the love, the life, he was offering. The world was at her feet, and it looked magnificent. If she had had no scruples, she would have let the answer that was in her heart pour forth without hesitation.

Rob smiled his encouragement. "Now it's your turn," he prompted her. "Simple, one-word answer."

Tip closed her eyes. "No," she whispered.

"That's not the one, sweetheart. Try again."

"I mean, no, there is no simple answer. There are things you don't know—"

"I know one thing," he interrupted brusquely, getting back to his feet. "I want to do this right. I want us to get married, and the sooner the better, after last night."

His obvious, and understandable, frustration only increased her pain. Knowing him as she did, Tip felt for him. After all, there was a shadow in his past, too. But right now, they had to deal with hers.

"I just asked you a question," he said, point-blank. "I think I deserve an honest answer."

"Rob, I don't know if I can marry you."

"You don't *know?*" She could hear the pain in his voice, as well as the disbelief. "Tip, what are you talking about?"

Before she could go on, he began to pace around the office. "Are you saying that I've been reading you wrong? That you meant something else, when you told me you loved me last night?"

"No," she said quickly. "It's not my feelings that I doubt. It's my ability to—" She paused, trying to gain control over her emotions. "To make it work," she finished.

He looked at her, his brows drawn together in concern. It was several minutes before he spoke.

"Tip, I'm just stunned. You and I have lived in the same house for weeks. We've taken things slow. We've gone through some good times, and some rough times. I've let you get closer to me than any other person has ever been or will ever be," he said, his blue eyes earnest. "Those are the things that make a marriage work. What in the world makes you think it wouldn't?"

"Past experience," she whispered.

His expression didn't change, but she saw something flicker in his eyes. "What are you talking about?" he said evenly.

Her heart threw itself against the walls of her chest. She steadied her voice as best she could. "Rob, I was married before. And divorced."

He took in a quick breath. She couldn't read the stark expression on his face, but imagined that it registered shock. When it finally came, his voice had a rough edge.

"How come you never told me before?"

The anger in his words made Tip's spine stiffen. "I thought it would be too painful," she said flatly. Then she added, in a whisper, "And I was right."

With that, Tip felt the instinct for self-preservation that had kept her running for five years roar back to life. She went out of the office door. When she was almost out of the garage, he called to her.

"Tip, wait," he said, his deep voice resonant in the empty space.

She kept walking. He caught up with her outside and placed his hand on her arm, his touch as light as the rain that had started to fall. She stopped. Gently, he turned her around to face him.

"What happened?" he asked, with quiet intensity. The look of raw emotion in his eyes pierced Tip right to her soul, despite herself.

"That shouldn't be too hard to guess," she said, with a bitter laugh. "I did what I do best. I left him."

It was raining harder now. Raindrops splashed into puddles on the driveway where they stood.

"Are you all right?" he asked her.

"Yes."

"Liar."

Startled, Tip found herself looking right into that intense blue gaze. But she was feeling too vulnerable to let him see too much, so she glanced away quickly.

"We need to resolve this thing." His voice held a commanding edge.

Tip opened her mouth, then shut it again. She really couldn't blame him for being upset. She *should* have told him before now. But how could she have known things would go so far? That he would have actually wanted her to be his wife, and Meredith's mother?

"I know," she said at last. She owed him that. Shivering in her damp clothes, she wrapped her arms around herself.

Rob swore under his breath. "Let's get back inside," he said, leading her into the office. He left her sitting on the sofa while he went to the storage closet for a couple of clean towels. Not only did they need to dry off—she needed time to pull herself together, and he needed time to process what he had heard.

It had knocked him for a loop, finding out that his woman had belonged to another man before. And that, close as they had become, as much as he had shared with her, as many opportunities to tell him as she had had, she had still chosen to keep this secret from him.

Try as he might, he couldn't think of one good reason why she should have held back on him. She *had* to know he would be interested in her previous marriage. Hell, he was interested in everything about her! It hurt to know she hadn't trusted him.

He went back and handed her a towel, dropping his on the floor. He bent down to pick it up, but that only reminded him that not long before, he had been on his knee right here on that same floor, making his proposal and anticipating his joy in her answer. But she hadn't said yes.

And, damn it all, *that* was what hurt most of all.

In defiance he sat on the floor, leaning back on his hands, his legs stretched out in front of him. His head tilted back slightly, so that he could hit her directly with his full blue gaze. "About your marriage," he said flatly.

Despite herself, Tip winced.

Rob's eyes narrowed for a moment as he registered her pain. Kind of how he felt. "Your marriage, and whatever ended it, obviously has a lot to do with your telling me you didn't know if you could marry me," he said.

Nodding, she cleared her throat. She knew he had been expecting a simple yes in answer to his proposal, and it had pained her to have to answer otherwise, to have to cause him pain.

"Saying I didn't know—Rob, that was the most honest answer I could give you."

"Tell me why," he said softly.

She took a deep breath. "You already figured out the part about my having a hard time getting men to see me—to see beyond the physical. And then Michael came along," she said. "Maybe because he was older, or because he had been my professor—I don't know—whatever the reason, I thought he was different. He treated me as his intellectual equal."

Rob almost choked on his next question, but he had to ask it. "Did you love him?"

She sighed. "I think you know me well enough to know the answer to that one."

Of course he did. Tip would never marry anyone that she wasn't in love with.

She wanted to say that her concept of love had been totally redefined since then. She had been so young, young enough to mistake fond regard for the kind of love that you base a lifetime on. But that would sound like she was making excuses. She kept her mouth shut.

Rob's expression hadn't changed at all. He looked completely detached from the conversation. His only answer was to get back to the original subject.

"But the marriage didn't work out," he said. He was trying to imagine a man getting Tip to love and marry him, and then letting her go. Despite himself, he felt his anger against this faceless ex-husband of Tip's begin to rise. "What did he do?"

"Nothing more than want his wife to be a wife to him," she said bluntly. "But I wasn't able to. That's why the marriage failed."

"Tip, what are you talking about?"

As dispassionately as she could, she told him about the breakup. About Michael's unexpected and persistent interest in the sexual part of the marriage, and her lack of response; about his wanting to do something about it, and her refusal.

Tip could tell that Rob wasn't fooled by her tone of detachment. She tried not to notice, but his clear blue eyes saw right through her. Her composure started to wear thin, so she hurried to finish. "So I left him. We got a divorce, and I went on with my life."

Rob suddenly jumped to his feet and began pacing around the room. "What life?" he said angrily. "The one that centers around the past that you have supposedly forgotten?"

Tip looked away quickly. "I don't know what you're talking about."

"No? What about the way you dress to hide your figure? What about the way you gave up a sport that you love, so no one would see you in a bathing suit?"

He paused, but she made no answer.

"What about your nightmares? What about the way you can't trust a man, because you're so afraid he can't see beyond your body? What about the way you live on the run?"

He stopped pacing and faced her, his eyes as hard as blue diamonds. "Have you really fooled yourself into thinking you don't have any regrets?"

She stood up to him. "Don't you dare talk to me about regrets, Rob Winfield. I regret every single one of those things. And more."

"You know what I regret?" he shot back. "I regret that you don't love me enough to be able to take a chance that I might be different from your ex-husband."

"I *know* you're different," she said angrily. "Can't you see? That's why, when you asked me to marry you, I had to admit that I didn't know if I could make it work. Because I didn't stick around to try to work things out the first time. I *left* my husband. And failing with Michael was one thing. Failing with you—well, you and Meredith deserve better than that."

"Damn right we do," he growled, and resumed pacing. He should have been upset to learn that Tip had run away from her marriage instead of trying to work at it. But that was another man, one she couldn't have loved like she loved him. And Rob loved her too much to give up on her because of a past mistake. The only way he would do that was if she left him and Meredith.

He took a deep breath. "Listen carefully, Tip," he said soberly, his eyes holding hers. "I have absolutely no doubt that you can satisfy me physically, as well as emotionally, intellectually, and every other way. I know that you have the temperament, the values, the capacity for love and caring to make our marriage work, and to be a wonderful wife to me and mother to Meredith." He paused. "*If* you can let the past be the past."

She could hardly believe it. He wasn't rejecting her after all. Rob knew everything, and he still wanted to marry her. He was leaving the choice up to her.

Tip bit her lip. Saying yes—how could she? He made it sound so easy, but there were so many potential difficulties that she couldn't just brush aside. She had been there. What if things didn't go so well? What if she would always be a leaver? How could she take that chance with Rob and Meredith? She loved them. *Really* loved them.

"Tip, it's up to you now," he said grittily.

Slowly, she walked over to the window, staring off into the distance. She had no right to keep him hanging. And she had no right to risk hurting him and his daughter.

She needed an answer—the right answer. The one in her heart was emphatic, but she was afraid that it was also selfish. As for her instincts, she was unable to read them for the doubts that clouded them. So she went with her intellect, which offered the only clear, rational choice. The one way she could be sure that she wouldn't let anyone down, or hurt anyone.

She swallowed the tears that were welling up in her throat. "I feel . . . I think it would be best if I left. For all of us."

Rob stared at her. Despite all the things she had walked away from in her past, he still hadn't thought she would walk away from his love.

But she was. And that told him all he needed to know.

He reached into his pocket and held out a set of keys. "Good timing," he commented dryly, dropping them into her palm. "You're running, and so is your car."

Without another word, without even looking at her, he took a deliberate step to one side, so that she could get past him to walk away.

Chapter Ten

Watching Tip walk away, Rob felt as if his heart were slowly, painfully, being pulled out by the roots. He couldn't believe she was actually leaving him. Not after all they had come to mean to each other. Not after they had said they loved each other.

But she had made her decision. And then he had made his. If she wanted to leave, fine. But he was not about to let her walk all over him on her way out of his life.

Rob popped open the hood of a car that was parked in the garage, and went to work. He needed to think, and he always did that best when his hands were busy.

He shouldn't be surprised, he tried to reason with himself. Tip had been leaving for years. How could he have expected her to stay with him?

But he'd *wanted* her to stay, dammit. He'd wanted her to stay and work things out, together. He'd wanted her to stay because she loved him. But there would have to be icicles in hell before he'd ask her to again.

He scraped his knuckle and it started bleeding. Cursing, he went into the office, washed his hand and held a cloth on it to stop the bleeding.

Letting Tip go was the only thing he could have done, for Meredith's sake. His daughter was young enough to be relatively unaffected by Tip's desertion. Far better now, than later. Those words reminded him of something he had once said to Tip about Sondra.

But somehow, it wasn't the same thing. At all.

Later, when Rob went to the house, Doc was in the kitchen, getting ready to give Meredith her supper.

Rob sat her down and started spooning cereal up for her. He needed something to do.

Doc leaned back against the kitchen counter, his arms crossed, watching. "Aren't you going to ask me where Tip went?" he asked finally.

Rob said nothing. It didn't much matter where Tip had gone. The fact was that she had chosen to leave.

Doc gave him a look of fatherly concern. "Well, she's packed up and gone. Where, she didn't say. Didn't say much of anything." He paused, but Rob kept feeding Meredith, methodically. Doc went on, quietly, "The fact is, son, when that woman walked out that door, she was in a world of hurt."

She was in a world of hurt? Rob wanted to yell. What about him?

This was it. It was all over. By leaving, she had done the one thing he could never get past. And she *knew* it. He was the last man in the world who would go running after a woman who had left him.

Meredith didn't need someone who took off when the going got tough, and neither did he. They needed a woman who would stand by them.

Rob didn't realize he had stopped feeding the baby until she started to bang her hands on the tray to get her next mouthful. He gave it to her, and noticed that Doc was looking away from him. But not because he didn't care.

Looking at his father standing there, caring but trying hard not to show it, made it easier for Rob to push aside the pride that was swelling up in him in the wake of his hurt. His stubborn pride had kept him away from people he cared about for long enough, and it had gotten him exactly nowhere. Tip had shown him his mistake—how ironic—and even though she was gone, he was not about to make that mistake again. Now, being by himself was the last thing he wanted, and not only because he would need Doc's help with the baby. Even more, he needed his father's friendship.

So he said to the man standing at the counter, "Want to stay for a while . . . Dad?"

Doc looked up and met his eyes. Then he went to the refrigerator and pulled out three bottles, two of beer and one of apple juice, and plunked them onto the table.

Not caring which direction she headed, Tip started putting miles between her and Madison. Between her and Rob. Between her and Meredith. Between her and the life she'd always wanted.

But what she wanted wasn't the most important thing, she reminded herself. By leaving Rob and Meredith, she was trying to do the right thing.

It was the hardest right thing she had ever done.

Once she had decided to do it, a numbness had overtaken her. It kept her, blessedly, beyond pain, beyond tears. The only sensory input she registered had to do with driving, and there was plenty of that, given that she was traveling on an unfamiliar highway in what was now a virtual downpour. The challenging road conditions were a welcome distraction.

When she came to a rest area, she pulled off and parked. As she rested her head on the steering wheel, the thought struck her that she had come full circle, and then some. This was where she had started out, after she had left her last job, when her car had broken down. Only now her car was working. Rob had probably finished it because of her interview, knowing she would need it if she got the job—and wanting to surprise her. Tears gathered behind her eyelids when she realized that he had even fixed the leak in the roof.

Blinking back her tears, she busied herself by reaching over into the passenger's seat, where she had thrown her purse and a pile of other things while she was hastily packing to leave. With any luck, her map would be there. She had to go somewhere, so she might as well get her bearings.

The map, it turned out, was at the bottom of the pile. Or not quite the bottom, she realized as she pulled it out. There was something under it.

When she saw what it was, Tip felt her breath catch. It was a single red rose, bruised and nearly crushed from the weight that had been on top of it. Rob, who had been planning on celebrating their engagement that evening, had no doubt put it there for her to find.

Well, she had found it, all right. With trembling hands, she picked it up and held it to her chest. And her tears finally flowed.

That evening, she stopped and checked into a little motel. It wasn't much, but it was quiet. A good place to settle in and do some work to get ready for her new job, she told herself.

Wearily, she unpacked her suitcase. Her movements were leaden, under the crushing weight of knowing that despite her good intentions, she had hurt Rob anyway. How had she ever let things go so far? She had told him she loved him—and then she had left.

Her deciding to leave was the one thing that was guaranteed to make him pull back and protect Meredith. She had been left before, and he was determined to keep his little girl from that kind of hurting.

Himself, too, Tip thought. She had seen too many facets of his sensitivity to believe that desertion by the woman he loved wouldn't be devastating for him.

But she'd *had* to go. One thing was still clear: better for her to take off now than after a marriage. Though she loved Rob, she was doing the best thing by leaving. And she was strong enough to go through with it.

She had to be. It was too late to change things, even if she wanted to.

All that week, Rob dropped Meredith off at day care and then worked with a vengeance. He growled every time anyone came near him, and that was only Fred and Ned, and only when it was clear they had no alternative. When the week began, he had had the foresight to tell them to take care of all dealings with customers, or he might have let this thing with Tip ruin his business, too.

While he banged around underneath a car one hot afternoon, he kept up a steady stream of swearing that was just below audible level in the rest of the garage.

Tip was gone. Gone for good. Rob had told himself a hundred times that her leaving *was* for the good. But he knew that if she had changed her mind and stayed, when those keys were in her hand, he would have taken her into his arms and never let go.

But she had chosen to leave. And at her decision, all his defensive instincts had surfaced, and he had circled the wagons around Meredith. Nothing was worth putting his daughter at risk for a big hurt.

One thing he had to admit, though. Rob had absolutely no doubt that Tip's feelings for his daughter were genuine. That put things in a different light, when he thought about her saying her leaving would be best for all of them. Because of her past, she had given him an honest answer when she had told him she didn't know if she could marry him.

Remembering the times her face had been aglow with genuine emotion for his baby gave him the overwhelming urge to chase after Tip, to convince her to come back, to take a chance that she would love him enough to stay.

But then he would think about his little angel, and know he couldn't. The chance wasn't his to take.

The noise he made working increased along with the volume of his swearing. If he still loved Tip, that was his tough luck. He would just have to get over it.

* * *

The days dragged by, hot and long. By Labor Day, Tip wished she had gone to Mary Kate's for the long weekend. She was all packed and ready to move the next day, when the apartment she had sublet would be available. Preparation for her classes, which also started on Tuesday, hadn't taken as long as she had expected, and there was nothing else to do, all alone in this little motel, but think about Rob. She was finding out that it had been far easier to leave than it was to let go.

Now that she had known Rob, she knew she would never be truly happy without him. She still wanted to live out her dream of marriage and a family, but only with him. And that was impossible.

She reminded herself that it would have hurt Rob—and Meredith—more, if she had run out on him after marrying him, as she had run out on her first marriage. She couldn't deny the fact that the divorce had been her idea. She hadn't tried to stay and work things out with Michael, to get counseling, as he had suggested.

But how could she have stayed? It was bad enough to be found lacking by her husband. She was mortified at the thought of having her sexual inadequacies analyzed and discussed by strangers.

And she now realized that there had been an even deeper, more compelling reason for her to dissolve her marriage vows. She had left because, somehow, she knew that no amount of discussion, or working on it, or counseling, could conjure up a feeling in her that she simply wasn't capable of feeling for Michael.

Tip had never consciously realized that before. She had been too busy feeling angry at him, disappointed in herself. She had clung to the illusion all these years that Michael had only wanted her for her body. Which, in all fairness, wasn't entirely true, although it had seemed that way at the time. It was right that two people who were married, and supposedly in love, should enjoy a strong physical attraction. In her marriage, there *was* something missing. That was why it had failed.

Physically, the heat she and Rob had created was enough to torch all those bad memories with Michael. Any inadequacy she had felt with her ex-husband was all in the past, all with him. And that experience might have made her *feel* like less of a woman, but, she had found out in Rob's arms, it didn't make her less of one. Rob had responded to her as passionately as she had to him.

But the memory of the passion she and Rob had shared was just that—a memory. And a torment. She needed to do something, go somewhere, anything to get her mind off of him. Tip was a walker, not a jogger, but when she put on her sneakers and headed down the road out front, she broke into a run.

She ran hard for several miles, much farther than she believed she was technically capable of running. But still it wasn't far enough, or fast enough.

Let the past...be the past, she chanted to herself as she ran. Rob had said it himself, and he was part of her past now.

But running from the past wasn't what he'd had in mind. As her feet pounded the pavement, understanding slowly dawned in Tip. More than anyone she had ever known, Rob had accepted his past and made the very best of it. Society at its most narrow-minded could condemn him for fathering a child out of wedlock, but not for abandoning that child. Meredith might not have been planned, but she was never unwanted. He loved her. Rob might not have asked to be a father, but he was a damned good one.

He had that quality that he had once said he was looking for in a woman—strength of character—and Tip now understood that that was a quality more desirable, more substantial, than strict morality. More gutsy than not trying because of fearing to fail.

She had thought she was being strong by leaving, by deciding it was best not to risk hurting Rob and Meredith. But really, that had never been hers to decide. He was the only one who could decide that. And he had been willing to take a chance on her—at least he had been until she had decided to leave.

In her heart, she had known that leaving her marriage was the right thing to do. At first she had felt guilty, yes. Maybe a little selfish. But regretful? Never. Her instincts had been right on target. She hadn't loved Michael, *really* loved him, after all. Leaving him had been painful, but it had felt right.

Leaving Rob, on the other hand, had all of her instincts screaming in protest. Even apart from him, Rob's pull was as strong as ever. Right now, she wanted to be in his arms, and more. She wanted a deeper connection with him.

Because what was missing in her marriage, she had found with Rob.

The realization hit her so hard, it took her breath away. Leaving Rob had been an intellectual decision; her heart had never been in it. Fear had overshadowed faith, and she hadn't been able to take a chance on telling him the heartfelt truth that she loved him, and wanted to stay with him forever.

She had never given him a simple, one-word answer to his proposal.

All of a sudden, she came to a stop. She stood still, swaying slightly on tired legs, breathing hard.

It was time to stop running.

It was time to stand and fight for what was worth fighting for. Her happiness. Her dreams. Her future.

And it was time to fight for Rob, the man who'd had more faith in her than she'd had in herself. Who had loved her so much, he had given her the freedom to choose to live without him.

She turned around and started running back toward the motel. She made it the whole way, without stopping.

The black-and-white sign that said Welcome to Madison slipped slowly past Tip's car. Apprehension gnawed at her insides as she made her way down the road past Ned and Fred's house. Fred, who was spending Labor Day afternoon washing the tractors, looked up as her car went slowly by. Recognizing her, he gave her a wide grin and an enthusiastic thumbs-up.

Tip's heart began to beat faster. Speeding up the car a fraction, she rounded a curve and saw Ned walking down the road, arm in arm with Susie. When he saw Tip's car, his jaw dropped. Then he jumped off the ground, thrusting a fist in the air as she drove past. In the rearview mirror, she watched as he grabbed Susie and gave her a passionate kiss. Tip couldn't help smiling. And stepping on the accelerator.

Labor Day was the official gathering of the Winfield family, although a couple of Rob's brothers had flown in early and spent the night at Doc's. Around noon on Monday, they started showing up at Rob's place.

Seeing his brothers provided only a meager distraction from his thoughts of Tip, but at least hosting the reunion kept him busy supplying everyone with food and drinks.

Doc was in charge of the baby, but every time Rob looked, a different one of his brothers was holding her and playing with her. Meredith's uncles adored her. Tip had been right.

While he was inside the house he heard Doc say, "Hello there! It's good to see you."

Rob wondered who his father was talking to, since all of his brothers were already there. He glanced out the window at the driveway. Parked at the end was Tip's car.

In slow motion, he walked out the back door.

He stood on the deck, watching. There was Tip, down at the pool, shaking hands with each of his brothers in turn as Doc made introductions. Rob was astounded. She had come back.

And not only that. She was wearing a bathing suit under a see-through mesh cover-up. For a woman whose longtime nightmare had been to have her body exposed in front of a group of men, that had taken guts.

He knew the exact moment when she realized he was standing there. She turned slowly, and her smile faded. Their eyes met, and locked.

After several heart pounds, she walked slowly toward him, as if the force between them was propelling her. She walked up the deck steps. In front of him, she stopped. They regarded each other warily.

"You're here," he said finally.

"I was invited," she blurted out, irrationally.

"That's not what I meant. I just never expected you would come."

"I promised you that I would if I could," she reminded him.

He gave a short laugh that was devoid of mirth. "Circumstances changed drastically since then."

"Some things never change," Tip said. After all, she still loved him. That hadn't changed, and never would. Even now, when he was looking at her with his blue eyes filled to the brim with stubborn pride.

Well, he was about to find out that she could be stubborn, too. She was through running, and she wasn't going to budge an inch. Begging and pleading wouldn't get through to him. There was only one way to convince him to give her another chance. She took her stance right in front of him, with her feet rooted firmly on the deck.

"A promise is a promise," she said.

"And leaving is leaving."

Pain flashed through Tip, but she squared her shoulders and stood her ground. "I thought it would be best. But I know now that I was wrong, Rob. I shouldn't have left."

He leveled his gaze at her in a wordless challenge. "So now you're back again," he finally said.

"Yes," she said, planting her fists solidly on her hips. "And this time, I'm here to stay."

"You think so?"

She couldn't miss the sarcasm in his question, but her answer was full of the confidence that was flowing deep within her.

"I *know* so," she said. "If I was strong enough to leave, loving you as I do, then I am certainly strong enough to stay."

He looked at her through narrowed eyes, but didn't say anything.

"I don't know what you're thinking, but I do know this," Tip warned. "If you want me to leave, you're going to have to fire up that old tow truck of yours and haul me out of here."

Rob felt his heart straining at the seams, as if one more swell of emotion would burst it wide open.

"Remember when I said you were a pain in the neck?" he said.

She nodded.

"You still are."

Her voice turned soft. "Remember when I said you'd miss me when I was gone?"

He made no answer, but reached into his pocket and pulled out a set of keys.

Curious, Tip watched him. He was concentrating on what he was doing, which was separating one key from the others on the key ring. At last, he looked up at her.

"If I ask you a simple question, do you think you can give me a simple, one-word answer this time?"

Tip nodded, not daring to hope. "What's the question?"

He looked at her assessingly. "Are you sure that the only way you'll ever leave is if I haul you out of here with the tow truck that uses this key?" he said, holding it up in the sunlight.

With all her heart, she gave him his simple, one-word answer.

"Yes."

Not looking away from her eyes, he tossed the key into the air and caught it in his fist. Then he went over to the deck railing, pumped his arm back and whipped the key far, far into the woods in back of his yard.

Tip watched it arc to a crest, shimmering as it turned end over end in the sunlight. When it fell, disappearing into the thick undergrowth, she looked at Rob. He was watching her from where he stood by the railing.

His intense blue gaze never wavering, he strode up next to her.

"That settles that," he said gruffly, and pulled her into his arms.

They kissed, a passionate kiss of love and healing, letting their lips tell of unspoken apologies and unconditional forgiveness, of aching regrets and fierce promises, of mistakes past and future and a bonding that transcended them all.

It was a long time before either one of them remembered that they weren't alone. They pulled apart, then Rob put his arm around Tip's shoulder, and slowly walked her down the stairs and across the backyard, to where his father and brothers sat talking by the pool. Everyone turned to look at them.

"Well, guys," Rob said to his family. "Think you'll be able to make it back for the wedding?"

After a noisy round of congratulations, Tip pulled away to go to Meredith, who was lying in her playpen, watching the grown-ups. When she caught sight of Tip, she started wiggling delightedly. Then she reached her tiny hands up to Tip.

Astonished, Tip turned to Rob. "When did she start doing that?"

"First I ever saw her do it," he said, his blue eyes shining with love and pride. "She must like the idea of you being her mommy as much as I do."

Tears flooded Tip's eyes as she picked the baby up and hugged her. She felt Rob's arms encircle them both, and lifted her face to his. Their lips met. And stayed.

* * * * *

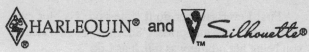

HARLEQUIN® and **Silhouette®**

are proud to present...

HERE COME THE GROOMS™

Four marriage-minded stories written by top
Harlequin and Silhouette authors!

Next month, you'll find:

A Practical Marriage	by Dallas Schulze
Marry Sunshine	by Anne McAllister
The Cowboy and the Chauffeur	by Elizabeth August
McConnell's Bride	by Naomi Horton

ADDED BONUS! In every edition of
Here Come the Grooms you'll find $5.00 worth
of coupons good for Harlequin and Silhouette
products.

On sale at your favorite Harlequin and Silhouette
retail outlet.

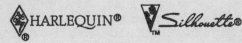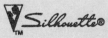

HARLEQUIN®   **Silhouette®**

HCTG896

Who can resist a Texan...or a Calloway?

This September, award-winning author
ANNETTE BROADRICK
returns to Texas, with a brand-new
story about the Calloways...

CLINT: The brave leader. Used to keeping secrets.

CADE: The Lone Star Stud. Used to having women
fall at his feet...

MATT: The family guardian. Used to handling
trouble...

They must discover the identity of the mystery
woman with Calloway eyes—and uncover a
conspiracy that threatens their family....

Look for **SONS OF TEXAS:** Rogues and Ranchers
in September 1996!

Only from Silhouette...where passion lives.

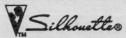

You can run, but you cannot hide...from love.

OUTLAWS and Lovers

This August, experience danger, excitement and love on the run with three couples thrown together by life-threatening circumstances.

Enjoy three complete stories by some of your favorite authors—all in one special collection!

THE PRINCESS AND THE PEA
by Kathleen Korbel

IN SAFEKEEPING
by Naomi Horton

FUGITIVE
by Emilie Richards

Available this August wherever books are sold.

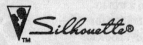

Silhouette®

Look us up on-line at:http://www.romance.net

SREQ896

FORTUNE'S Children™

Bestselling Author
LISA
JACKSON

Continues the twelve-book series—FORTUNE'S CHILDREN
in August 1996 with Book Two

THE MILLIONAIRE AND THE COWGIRL

When playboy millionaire Kyle Fortune inherited a Wyoming
ranch from his grandmother, he never expected to come
face-to-face with Samantha Rawlings, the willful woman
he'd never forgotten...and the daughter he'd never known.
Although Kyle enjoyed his jet-setting life-style, Samantha and
Caitlyn made him yearn for hearth and home.

MEET THE FORTUNES—a family whose legacy is greater than
riches. Because where there's a will...there's a *wedding!*

A CASTING CALL TO
ALL FORTUNE'S CHILDREN FANS!
If you are truly one of the fortunate
few, you may win a trip to
Los Angeles to audition for
Wheel of Fortune®. Look for
details in all retail Fortune's Children titles!

Look us up on-line at: http://www.romance.net